★

"WELL, AS FAR AS I UNDERSTAND IT,"

Hooky said when his Aunt had finished outlining the scenario, "I've got to do a reforming act. I might as well buy myself a tambourine and join the Salvation Army."

"I very much doubt if they would have you. For once in a way, Hooky, you have a chance of doing something sensible, something constructive; there is a young girl, and I don't doubt she is an attractive young girl, involved; and equally I have no doubt that Leo Chanderley will act handsomely in the matter of a present or fee if you want to be coarse."

"I can seldom resist the temptation to be coarse," Hooky said smiling at his Aunt.

★

"An exuberent adventure."

—*Times Literary Supplement*

Also available from Worldwide Mystery by
LAURENCE MEYNELL

DON'T STOP FOR HOOKY HEFFERMAN

A Forthcoming Worldwide Mystery by
LAURENCE MEYNELL

THE FAIRLY INNOCENT LITTLE MAN

HOOKY GETS THE WOODEN SPOON

LAURENCE MEYNELL

WORLDWIDE®

TORONTO • NEW YORK • LONDON • PARIS
AMSTERDAM • STOCKHOLM • HAMBURG
ATHENS • MILAN • TOKYO • SYDNEY

HOOKY GETS THE WOODEN SPOON

A Worldwide Mystery/August 1991

This edition is published by arrangement with Scarborough House.

ISBN 0-373-26077-6

Printed in U.S.A.

CONTENTS

ONE

Sale of a masterpiece

THE CLOCK over the vast fireplace in the Club smoking room announced the afternoon hour with three tinny strokes...

Leo Chanderley automatically checked with the old-fashioned half-hunter which he had inherited from his father, and indeed from his grandfather.

The half-hunter agreed that it was three o'clock. Sir Leo Chanderley's companion—the two men had been drinking post-luncheon coffee together—noticed the movement and said, 'I expect you've got plenty to do, with this wedding coming off.'

Chanderley didn't care much for the man, one of the newer members and a bit of a 'thruster', but civility as from one club member to another was demanded. Leo Americ Chanderley was a great believer in civility.

'Oh yes, there's a lot of preparation,' he agreed. 'But I must admit I leave most of it to my wife. She's pretty competent, you know.'

As he said this he smiled slightly. He had a mental image of Lois. Tall; too thin perhaps to be really beautiful, but with breeding stamped all over her; still suffering from the tragedy of eighteen months ago; worried to death about Virginia; but quite determined that Rachel's wedding was going to be all it ought to be; up to standard. Lois Chanderley, the grand-daughter of a Duke, had been brought up with a regard for standards. Competent indeed.

'Let's see, your eldest daughter, isn't it?' The question sought no information; the thruster was perfectly well aware of the answer to it; his query was designed simply to remind Sir Leo Chanderley in an oblique way that he needn't be so high and mighty and stand-offish since quite a few people knew he was having trouble with his second girl. Time to put the thruster down a bit Chanderley decided.

'My *elder,*' he answered. 'I have only two.' *And ask about the second one if you dare,* the final words were not spoken, but they were there; they hung discernibly in the air.

The thruster did not quite dare. Instead: 'I think I'll see if there's a game of bridge going,' he said and disappeared into the card room.

Three members were sitting at a table waiting. Their bridge-hungry eyes lit up at the arrival of a fourth. As the cards were being dealt the newcomer said, 'Just been talking to Leo Chanderley. *Sir* Leo. A bit of a dry old stick.'

'That business of his boy a year or so ago must have hit him pretty hard,' the dealer said.

'And then there's all the nonsense that girl of his gets up to.'

The thruster gathered up his cards and gave a short laugh. 'He doesn't like to talk about that,' he said, 'and no wonder.'

Dyke, doyen of Club hall porters, helped Sir Leo on with his overcoat, and did it properly, not failing to put a hand up underneath to tug down the suit jacket in case it had ridden up out of place.

The attention pleased Chanderley; not many club servants take the trouble to do that nowadays, he thought.

'Thank you, Dyke.'

'Nice bright day, Sir Leo; but a nip in the air all the same. Everything going all right for the wedding?'

Chanderley nodded. 'You know what these things are,' he said. 'Awful lot of fuss and flapdoodle but the ladies glory in it all.'

The two men smiled at one another, a masculine smile; man to man stuff. Where should we be without the ladies, God bless 'em . . .

'I expect everything will be all right on the day,' Sir Leo added hopefully and he went out through the club entrance down the four shallow stone steps and into the bright sunshine of a London afternoon.

It was too early to go back to Eaton Square for tea so, even if you were constantly lamenting that the West End wasn't what it used to be, why not a stroll up Bond Street to see what, if anything, remained of elegance?

Bond Street was on its best behaviour and it turned out to be surprisingly rewarding. Patched jeans and scruffy pullovers were noticeably absent; starched formality might have gone, but the casualness that had taken its place undeniably had its own attractiveness.

Sir Leo walked slowly, stopping every now and again when his eye was caught by a piece of fine furniture in some dealer's window. He was thus engaged, looking at a superb, if somewhat too ornate, Louis XIV marquetry bureau when, unknown to him, he was spotted by a woman coming down the street in the opposite direction.

This woman was twenty-four years old; she was long-legged and rangy, making you think that in her teens she had probably been called *gawky;* she was not wearing a hat, so that her hair was in some disorder; she walked with a very slight limp because she had been born with a defect in her right foot. She was Virginia Chanderley, the younger daughter of the man now appraising the marquetry bureau and thinking, at the back of his mind, how comforting it was to reflect that, if he really wanted the thing and if Lois would find room for it in the already overcrowded drawing room in Eaton Square, he could afford even the extravagant price tag attached to it.

It was more than a year since Virginia had seen her father; she had no desire to meet him now: she found it hard to feel any affection for the man whose loins had brought her into the world; she could think of him only as representing all that she imagined she must get away from.

She was near enough to see what he was doing... *buying more furniture,* she thought, *God Almighty, haven't they got enough already in the damned drawing room? Won't they ever learn anything?...*

It was clear that in a moment she and her father would meet and she didn't want that to happen. She took the nearest way out; she turned, and merely with the idea of avoiding an awkward moment, went into Christie's.

Instantly she was surrounded by the all-pervading atmosphere of money. The feeling of money was in the air. People were there with treasures to sell, desperately anxious for a good price as a life-line out of many difficulties; others, convinced that money was rapidly becoming worthless, were there to get rid of the stuff and translate it into something durable that would retain its value; a small section who could still put their hands on all the money they wanted, were there with the fanatical lust of the collector burning in their calculating eyes.

The acolytes of the temple—polished young women, almost extravagantly well-dressed young men—were busy everywhere; their speech and manners reflecting the civilized nature of the objects they handled daily.

'Thank God I don't work here,' was Virginia's typical reaction to them; it occurred to her that she might have made a mistake in her swift choice of a bolt hole; it was quite possible, after all, that her father had been heading for Christie's himself; but when she gained the actual sale-room she saw that this was not likely since not furniture but pictures were being sold.

'....six, then, I am bid. The bid is on my right, gentlemen, at six thousand...I don't want to protract the proceedings—' the Auctioneer's eyes ran over his congregation. He had already sized them up even before the first lot had been offered. Very much the standard mixture he had decided. Fifty per cent of them of no account at all, sightseers only; fascinated by merely hearing huge sums of money mentioned; terrified lest some inadvertent nod or gesture might be construed as a bid; storing up material for the evening gossip: *'my dear, I was in Christie's this afternoon—oh yes, I often pop in there—and you've no idea...'*

Then there were perhaps thirty per cent 'market followers', zealously annotating their catalogues, keeping tabs on what was sold, who bought it and at what price, the work-horses of the trade. Another ten per cent the Auctioneer reckoned as 'possibles', there might well be a bid from them, if not for the most expensive lots at any rate for something in the more moderate range. This left the ten per cent who mattered; the ones who had come there to buy if possible and at any rate to bid and to bid high. All these the Auctioneer knew by sight. He knew not only what they all looked like, he knew also what their individual preferences were; he generally knew whom they were representing if they came on behalf of a client; he could make a very shrewd guess at how much each of them was prepared to go to for any individual lot.

'. . . I don't want to protract the proceedings,' he said. 'Has anybody anything to say over six thousand?'

Nobody had anything to say over six thousand; the little ivory gavel rapped decisively on the Auctioneer's desk and he said *'Sold'*, adding in an undertone the name of the purchaser to his assistant who was already entering the details in his book.

The next lot, a winter scene in Holland—the sale was almost exclusively of Dutch paintings—was put up, bid for and sold for fourteen thousand pounds, in three minutes flat.

'Fourteen thousand quid in three minutes,' Virginia told herself. 'They must all be insane.'

She studied the insane ones, the three dozen or so people filling the two front rows of seats where she judged most of the bidding was coming from.

Many of the bids she had not been able to detect; occasionally she spotted the flick of a catalogue, or a hardly perceptible nod that would send the price up by five hundred pounds.

The conventional conspiratorial secrecy confirmed her conviction that the whole thing had something rotten about it and young Virginia was good at detecting rottenness in the state of Denmark.

'If they are fools enough to be willing to spend all that money on the thing why the devil don't they open their mouths and say so?' she contemptuously wondered, 'instead of all this hugger-mugger nonsense of nods and becks?'

Roddy ought to be here studying this lot, she thought, it would help him in his acting; there was one figure in particular who caught her attention: an untidily dressed man sitting hunched up towards the middle of the front row. Looking at him your eye was first of all irresistibly drawn to his astonishing headgear. Why he should be wearing anything at all on his head in that overheated room was difficult to understand and that anyone would deliberately choose a thing that looked like an unhappy cross between a Tam o'shanter and an over-sized beret was astonishing—'a nut case, like the rest of them,' Virginia summed up in her dismissive way.

The Auctioneer didn't think that the man in the centre of the front row was a nut case; nor was he surprised by that extraordinary piece of headgear; he knew it well; he knew the wearer of it well—Julius Bern who was so wealthy that the old-fashioned term millionaire was hardly adequate to describe him. An eccentric. And a very difficult customer to handle in the sale-room. Touchy. Do or say anything, however innocent, which the little, shrivelled up figure could somehow construe as hostile or derogatory and he would be liable to shut up like a clam. No bids out of him that day. But catch him on a good day (and nobody ever knew what constituted a good day for Julius Bern) and he would probably go on bidding until he got what he had made up his mind to get.

'Lot thirty-three,' the Auctioneer announced, and a slight but unmistakable rustle of excitement and expectation ran through the room. This was the item they had all been waiting for; now they would hear real money talked about.

'*Woman with a Flageolet* by van Dysen the Elder; it isn't necessary, ladies and gentlemen, for me to dilate on the virtues of this painting, nor to say anything about its provenance, which is quite impeccable as we all know that the picture has been in the same ducal house since it was first painted in 1632. I shall merely ask you therefore to start the bidding for me. Fifty shall I say? Shall I say fifty thousand?... thank you; fifty I'm bid, on my right—'

'One hundred and fifty thousand.'

Julius Bern's high-pitched voice, almost a squeak, took the Auctioneer by surprise; the multimillionaire's usual way of signalling his bids was so deliberately furtive that you had to be very wide awake not to miss them. The size of the bid and the unexpected way in which it was made sent a buzz round the room... had the old devil really got his shooting boots on and would he go on bidding till ultimately he got the picture? Or had he already made up his mind that a hundred and fifty thousand was his top figure and would he now shut up tight-lipped and not utter another word?

The man on the rostrum weighed these two equal possibilities in his mind and had no idea which would turn out to be correct. If the bid of a hundred and fifty thousand was designed to knock out a certain number of lesser fry who might hopefully have stayed in for a round or two it succeeded; but Blanchard, from the New York gallery, wouldn't be intimidated by it of course; the question was what was it safe to up the bids by? The Auctioneer decided on twenty-fives.

'One hundred and fifty thousand I'm bid; thank you, Mr Bern.' (Julius Bern glowered, he hated his name being used in public.) 'Shall I say one hundred and seventy-five thousand?'

He glanced towards the extreme left of the second row where a man sat wearing heavily rimmed glasses. Weston Blanchard of New York whose gallery specialised in the Dutch School would be likely to want anything by either of the van Dysens, but especially the Elder.

Blanchard's system of bidding was well-known to the Auctioneer; when he touched his glasses it was a bid; when he took his glasses off and began to polish them with his handkerchief he had finished. Now outstretched forefinger and thumb went up to re-adjust the glasses on the bridge of his nose.

'One hundred and seventy-five thousand I'm bid; may I put it up to two hundred thousand?'

'No you may not. Not for me,' the squeaky voice said in obvious irritation. 'One hundred and eighty thousand.'

'Thank you, thank you. One hundred and eighty thousand—'

The hand went up to the glasses again.

'One hundred and eight-five—' the Auctioneer said.

'One hundred and ninety thousand.'

'And five thousand more on my left, one hundred and ninety-five thousand.'

'Two hundred thousand,' from Bern.

The Auctioneer's eyes darted to the end of the second row; there was a slight hesitation but finally the glasses were touched once more.

'Two hundred and five thousand I am bid on my left.'

'Two hundred and fifty thousand.'

'I beg your pardon, Mr Bern, did I hear your bid correctly?'

'I thought I spoke clearly enough,' Julius Bern squeaked irritably. 'I bid two hundred and fifty thousand pounds.'

The man from New York did some quick thinking; the dollar was still strong against the pound, of course, but even so he reckoned he was now out of his depth; in his memory a van Dysen had never fetched anything like a quarter of a million pounds before and he doubted if one ever would again. If this eccentric old English fossil wanted to throw his money about, good luck to him. Weston Blanchard was a great bridge player and he knew when to say 'no bid'. He took off his glasses and began to polish them on his handkerchief.

'For the last time,' the Auctioneer said, 'two hundred and fifty thousand pounds.' He gave a token glance round the room, waited for the conventional five seconds and then rapped smartly with his ivory gavel.

Instantly a hubbub of talk broke out. People were intrigued and amused. The knowledgeable ones wondered whether Julius Bern had overshot the mark, or whether with the infallible instinct of the really rich he had got himself on to a good thing; the ones not qualified to debate that point still buzzed with excitement; they had seen a small oblong of painted canvas (62 cm by 45 cm the catalogue said) change hands for a quarter of a million pounds, and even in these degenerate days that sounded like a lot of money to most of them.

Virginia got back to Stanmere Gardens at half past four. The day had turned unreasonably warm and her foot was beginning to throb a little. She had occupied herself on the way by going over her part in a but recently launched play. It wasn't a big part, but she was on in all three acts and had a speech of a couple of dozen lines just before the curtain of act two.

...of course if you really think the matter can be settled...only it wasn't *'settled'* it was *'arranged'*; of course if you really think the matter can be *arranged*— somehow she could never be sure of getting it right; *'settled'* came automatically to her lips; as soon as she had said it she knew it was wrong and

that threw her out of her stride for the rest of her opening speech.

She had been lucky to get the part. She knew that; but she probably didn't realise how lucky.

'O.K.' the producer had said, 'there's only the girl's part we haven't settled then.'

'What about Virginia Cave?' (Virginia Chanderley's stage name).

The producer made a face. 'She might do. She'd be adequate I suppose.'

'The part calls for someone with a limp and she's got one naturally.'

'As long as she doesn't get up to any of her political tricks; these women who get bitten with the revolutionary bug are just a plain bloody nuisance. I want actresses not god-damned politicians.'

'She's got the looks and a certain amount of ability and we shan't have to pay her all that much.'

'O.K. O.K. Give her a try. Limited contract of course. If she makes a nuisance of herself we'll get rid of her.'

As far as Virginia was concerned the offer had come unexpectedly. Out of the blue. And of course it had made Roddy as sick as mud with jealousy. Roddy had had ideas about going on the stage himself; he had had ideas about going into Fleet Street; about being a writer; about doing something in the P.R. line. He felt perfectly sure that if he had wanted to he could have succeeded in any of these worlds, but he just couldn't be bothered to want to (or so he told himself); there were other, less demanding things to be interested in; there were soothing cigarettes to be rolled and smoked; there were the women who so conveniently fell for him; there was good old Social Security...

Stanmere Gardens.

The 'Gardens' part was a bit of a misnomer. A euphemism. It referred to a strip of tired looking grass at the back of the block of flats where boys kicked footballs about; there was a dustbin or two to be seen; an unappetising selection of the general detritus of human existence was generally lying around.

At the bottom of the stone staircase which gave access to all the flats in the block Virginia encountered a short dumpy figure dressed in black. She knew who he was and although she had never spoken to the man in her life she managed to hate him. He was Father Frederick Smith, the priest in charge of the local Catholic parish of St Jude; he had been visiting an old woman in one of the ground floor flats and he was now going back to the presbytery where, he hoped, the cake for afternoon tea would not be as stale as it so often was. As far as Virginia was concerned the inoffensive little man was Religion; which was why she hated him...*all that love of God stuff* she often exclaimed angrily *how can anybody fall for it; just look at the world...*

A man came out of flat 6 just as Virginia reached the third floor. He passed her on the stairs and they exchanged quick enquiring glances, but neither spoke. The man had a scar running across the right cheek of a deeply lined face.

Inside the flat the air was stale; the smell of tobacco smoke hung about and the untidy remains of a scrap midday meal—two unwashed plates and a beer bottle—littered the table. A transistor set was turning out noise. Roddy Marten was sitting in front of the single bar electric fire, his sandalled feet on the seat of a chair; he was wearing green corduroy trousers and a grubby yellow pullover. You might have thought that nobody in their senses could have seen anything attractive about him; but Virginia Chanderley, now aged twenty-four, intelligent, quick-witted, ex-Roedean and Eaton Square, was not in her senses where this particular man was concerned; but even her temporary obsession about him was beginning to wear thin.

'Who was that who just went out?' she asked.

'Mind your own business. He calls himself Len Carron if it's of any interest to you. Where have you been? Rehearsing this wonderful play of yours?'

Even if she had been at rehearsal Virginia would probably not have said so; it would have stirred

Roddy's jealousy and made him more bad tempered than he obviously was.

'Actually I've been in Christie's. Who is Len Carron anyway?'

'Christie's? The place in Bond Street? What in God's name were you doing there?'

No point, she decided, in explaining exactly why. 'I was in Bond Street with nothing much to do and I just went in on an impulse.'

'Did you buy anything?' Roddy enquired facetiously.

'Buy anything? What with? I watched other people buying, bidding, for a bit. God Almighty, Roddy, the money there is knocking about. Thousands bid every few seconds, just like that.'

'Len Carron has got one or two ideas for getting hold of some money.'

'Such as?'

'Never mind, nothing to do with you. Just some business we were talking over together.'

'How did he get that scar on his face?'

'In Durham jail if you must know; but I wouldn't ask him about it. By the way, a letter came for you by the second post.'

The transistor set continued its cacophony unheeded; the man and the woman were so used to the noise that they didn't even notice it.

'It has been opened,' Virginia commented.

'Of course it has been opened. I opened it. I wanted to see whom it was from. I thought it might be one of your many admirers.'

The girl flushed slightly but said nothing.

'And will you be going to this fashionable function?' Roddy enquired.

Virginia was studying the contents of the envelope: a gilt-edged imposing card inviting her to the wedding of... *their daughter Rachel to Commander Ronald St John Dellington, R.N.* and a covering letter from her mother.

'What a lot of flapdoodle,' Virginia said.

'And you'll be going to it?'

The girl gave a quick hard laugh. 'I might. It could be rather fun in a way, seeing them go through all the same old antics.'

TWO

'Like a bleeding duchess'

MRS MASON'S unvarying tipple in the Spotted Dog (officially known as The Talbot) was a double port with a dash of gin in it; fortified by a couple of these sustaining draughts she was apt every evening to dilate to her cronies about her own remarkable virtues and the circumstances of her life.

'. . . wouldn't know what to do without me the old lady wouldn't,' was one of her frequent assertions. 'Course in times past she was one of the hoity-toity sort, used to ring for her butler to tell the second footman to tell the page boy to get to hell out of it. We all know that. But that was in times past, wasn't it? Now it's Ada Mason, two hours a day and lucky to get me. I can pick and choose. I'm not unreasonable, mind you. And I know a lady when I see one. Sits there like a bleeding duchess, she does. *Mrs Mason this and Mrs Mason that*. . . oh dear, oh dear, lives in the past the poor old soul does. Of course I just get on with my work regardless and if there's a bit of pickings when it comes to knocking off time and she isn't looking, well that's the way of things, isn't it?

God helps them as helps themselves as the saying goes...'

The Honourable Theresa Page-Foley, who did not frequent the Spotted Dog, gave a slightly different account of the relations between herself and her daily woman. Nobody was quite sure of Theresa Page-Foley's exact age; she might have been seventy-eight, she might have been eighty-seven; the best bet was that she was somewhere in between. As a young woman she had seen the heyday of the thing; the grouse-moor, yachts and Royal Enclosure at Ascot era; but heydays have a habit of passing. Heydays don't survive little affairs like the Battle of the Somme; and for Theresa Page-Foley a twelve-roomed country house in the Home Counties had given place to a two-roomed flat in Hove.

Circumstances might have changed but Mrs Page-Foley herself had changed very little. Age had merely served to fortify her conviction that the majority of her fellow humans were fools and the rest dishonest. The one thing she never allowed herself to indulge in was self-pity.

'I am an extremely fortunate woman,' she was apt to tell her friends. 'I've got everything I want in two rooms; a good deal more than I want, really, and it's such a relief not to have to worry about eight indoor servants and four gardeners and just to have this one woolly-witted creature who comes in daily and does the donkey work. Of course she's incompetent; but then who isn't these days? Blessed are the Incompetent for they shall inherit Social Security. Actually I don't let her touch any of the valuable things. I just sit there whilst she's threshing about and keep an eye on her and when it's time for what she calls "knocking off" I look the other way so that she can do her bit of pilfering without either of us being embarrassed.'

Mrs Page-Foley was thus engaged one bright April morning, sitting bolt upright on a hard chair and keeping a wary eye on Mrs Mason to make sure that she didn't touch any of the Crown Derby plates when the telephone rang.

Mrs Mason, who happened to be immediately next to the instrument, answered it. She dealt with it cautiously having never fully got over a suspicious mistrust of the thing. Eventually she was able to announce, 'There's a gentleman talking down this thing, um, as would like to speak to you.'

There were very few people in the world whom Ada Mason addressed as *um*; Mrs Page-Foley was one of them.

Theresa Page-Foley had imagined that the call would be from one of her bridge-playing woman acquaintances, 'the bird-witted three no-trumps Hove lot' as she was wont to describe them; but, a gentleman...!

Rising a little awkwardly from her chair, walking a little stiffly across the room, she smiled slightly. She had been thinking of times past and this fitted aptly with her thoughts. In those days long gone the Mayfair telephone was always ringing; Venables the archdeacon-like butler was always announcing 'Miss Theresa, a gentleman to speak to you . . .'

'Is that Mrs Page-Foley?'

'It is.'

'Theresa, this is Leo Chanderley speaking—'

'Leo!'—a voice from the past indeed! 'Where on earth are you, Leo?'

'At Brighton railway station.'

'At the railway station?'

'I caught the eleven o'clock from Victoria—I'm running away from Lois.'

'Good heavens—'

A chuckle reassured her. 'No, no, no. Not really. Not in a thousand years. What I mean is that Lois doesn't know that I'm down here. As a matter of fact when I left Eaton Square this morning I didn't know myself that I was coming down. I was on my way to the club as usual and then I suddenly thought damme, it's a nice sunny day and a breath of sea air will do me a world of good so why not catch the eleven from Victoria and have a look at Brighton; and, on the journey down, I remembered that you live somewhere in these parts and I could do with a little advice—'

'Advice, Leo?'

'I'll tell you when I see you. I've got your address from the telephone book; somewhere in Hove isn't it?'

'In what my disreputable nephew calls darkest Hove.'

'Will it be all right if I call on you?'

'Leo, it will be like a ray of sunshine from the long ago. Nowadays I'm an old woman and rather a lonely one and I can't tell you how pleased I shall be to see you.'

'I'll get a cab and be with you in ten minutes or so.'

Mrs Mason, who always listened unashamedly to any conversation on the telephone, was vastly intrigued.

'Someone is coming to see you, um?' she enquired.

'Sir Leo Chanderley is on his way here.'

'A gentleman visitor! That's nice for you, um. I always say a gentleman caller makes all the difference—they're a lot of trouble, mind you, but then they're a lot of fun too, and you can't have one without the other, can you? Shall I make you a nice pot of tea before I go, um?'

Mrs Page-Foley declined the offer of a nice pot of tea and after shooing her daily woman out of the flat considered—dry sherry? Madeira? or a half bottle of Moet et Chandon?

Eventually she filled the sink with cold water, stood a half bottle of Moet et Chandon in it and put a few biscuits on a plate.

When Leo Chanderley arrived and Theresa opened the door to him the two human beings, the man and the woman, stood stock-still for a moment making frank assessment of each other. Once inside and sitting down Chanderley said, 'Well, well, well, it's been a long time—all of thirty years, must be.'

'More like forty, my dear man.'

'*Eheu fugaces,* I'm not sure that they do Latin any more at Harrow but I still remember a tag or two.'

'I never saw the slightest use in Latin,' Mrs Page-Foley said briskly.

Sir Leo laughed. 'You were always pretty downright Theresa,' he said, 'that was one of the things I liked about you.'

'Still I must admit that Harrow doesn't seem to have done you any harm; you're a highly successful man, Leo. If you haven't forgotten how to open a bottle of champagne we can drink to one another's health, if indeed that is a suitable thing to do at my age; instead let's drink to confusion to the barbarians.'

Chanderley had not forgotten how to open a bottle of champagne and when their two glasses had been charged and the suggested toast duly drunk he reverted to a remark of a few minutes earlier.

'Successful? Well, yes, in a way I have been. It would be silly to deny it. But you remember what Doctor Johnson said—'

'I haven't the vaguest idea what that scrofulous old bore said, and if I had I'm sure I should disagree with it. I regard him as a tedious old moralist of polysyllable sentences and revolting habits.'

'It would have been interesting to hear the two of you together. I wonder what odds the bookies would have given on the outcome. Still in spite of your prejudices, the old boy did occasionally hit the target as, for instance, when he said that the great aim of every man was to be happy at home.'

Theresa Page-Foley took a sip of champagne and considered...was she being asked to take part in the classic situation? Had Leo Chanderley come down to Hove to tell her that there was a rift within the lute? To complain that Lois didn't really understand him?

He cut short these speculations with his next words. 'For heaven's sake don't even begin to think that there is anything wrong between Lois and me. As I told you on the telephone, not in a thousand years. Lois is an all-time topnotcher; a thoroughbred. You probably know that we have two daughters?'

'Yes, I remember hearing that; but we've been out of touch for so long now that I've no idea what's happened to the girls; are they married or what? I don't even know their names.'

'Rachel and Virginia. I've Jewish blood in my ancestry of which I am very proud, so I like the name Rachel. She's the elder by the way; rising twenty-seven and due to be married very shortly.'

'Congratulations. And are you happy about that?'

'Very happy. A fellow called Dellington. Ronald St John Dellington. A Commander in the Navy. All very suitable and proper. Lois and I are both very happy about that.'

'And the other girl? Virginia?'

Leo Chanderley took a mouthful of champagne, swirled it appreciatively round his palate and eventually swallowed it. He stared hard at his hostess and shook his head in a despairing sort of way.

'That's what I've come to see you about, Theresa. What the devil goes wrong? Between parents and children, I mean. I love both those girls, of course; I know it's wrong to have a favourite, but still I've always felt that there was something special between me and the younger one, Virginia—Ginny—she's just twenty-four now.'

'And what is she doing?'

'Doing?' Chanderley spread his hands. 'God knows what she's doing, or whom she's doing it with.

It's quite obvious *she* doesn't think there is anything special between us because she can't stand the sight of me. Or of her mother. Or of her home. She simply contracted out; went away; on her own—well, unfortunately not on her own. She's got herself mixed up with a most undesirable lot. I don't know the details. I can't get near the girl. She won't let me. I'm not even sure where she's living, but every now and again bits of news come back to us in a roundabout way which make both her mother and myself desperately afraid. She seems to have taken up with a Left-Wing lot of extremists, practically revolutionaries as far as I can make out and God alone knows what will come of it.'

'Is there a man mixed up in this?' Mrs Page-Foley asked, adding in her tart fashion, 'There usually is when a woman begins to act like a congenital idiot. I sometimes wonder if the Almighty knew what he was doing when he created male and female. We should all have been spared so much trouble if he had been content with just one sex.'

'Maybe there is a man. I suppose there probably is. But I'm not sure about it. It may be just a sort of wild idealism. Ginny's bitten with this revolutionary bug that seems to get all the young these days. She just wants to pull everything down; according to her everything our generation did was bad.'

'The worst thing our generation did was to breed children like the present lot,' Mrs Page-Foley said.

'Then of course there was the frightful business of Alec—'

'What was that?'

Sir Leo drained his glass and held it out to be replenished. 'A bit humiliating to think how we come to rely on this stuff to pull us through,' he said with a wry little laugh.

'Tell me about Alec.'

'Our boy. Killed in Northern Ireland eighteen months ago. In the Royal East Staffords. Twenty-six years old. The apple of his mother's eye; and of Ginny's too. When he was blown up it knocked her off balance completely. Ranted and raved. The whole thing in Ireland was monstrous and wicked. The English ought not to be there at all. The whole business of war was wicked. Lois and I were wicked ever to have sent Alec to Sandhurst and so into the Army. We were responsible for the boy's death—you've never heard anything like it and the dreadful part was that in a way, up to a point, I could sympathise with the girl. I knew what she was feeling; God Almighty, wasn't I the boy's father? Wasn't I feeling it myself? But I couldn't get near her. I couldn't say anything that she would listen to. She stormed out of the house; stormed out shouting "you're all rotten, the lot of you, the whole thing's rotten," banged the door behind her and left her mother and me in tears—Lois crying, imagine!'

'So what now, Leo?' Theresa asked gently.

'I'm desperately anxious to save the girl. I know she's twenty-four. I know everyone is supposed to be grown up and worldly-wise and sophisticated these days before they are out of the nursery; but of course it isn't like that at all really. In many ways Ginny is only a kid. I can't help thinking of her as a kid anyway; and God knows what will become of her if we can't get her away from the sort of life she is leading and the sort of people she has taken up with. But I don't know how to do it. I simply do not know how to do it. You can imagine that Lois and I have talked about this till our throats are sore. Without getting any further. We neither of us know what to do. And now Lois won't even talk about it. I think she has been too hurt, what with Alec being blown up and Ginny turning against her—my God, who would be a woman, a mother, eh? So I have nobody to talk it over with. Then this morning, as I told you when I rang up, walking from Eaton Square in the sunshine I suddenly thought to hell with business in the City, I want some fresh air, what about a visit to Doctor Brighton—and in the train this marvellous idea came to me—*Brighton,* I thought, *why Theresa Page-Foley lives down there somewhere and she's just the sort of person I could talk this over with*—so here I am, my dear, all the happier for seeing you again and for having got the whole thing off my chest; and I promise not to say another word about it.'

'Nonsense,' Mrs Page-Foley said sharply. 'Of course we shall say another word about it. All my life I have taken the greatest pleasure in telling other people what they ought to do and how they should organise their lives. We must get in touch with this silly girl of yours—'

'*How?*—my dear Theresa I pose the one simple question to you *how?* We've got an address which may or may not be right; and even if it is right and if I went round there I'm quite sure I wouldn't be admitted. Possibly she's living with a crook, or in some sort of commune. I suppose she goes into coffee bars and discotheques—what is a discotheque anyway? A gramophone in a dingy basement as far as I am concerned. You can see how hopelessly out of touch I am; it's simply not my scene as they say nowadays; it's not water I can swim in.'

'Then we must employ somebody whose scene it is, who can swim in it.'

'My dear Theresa, it's easy to say these things—'

'What about your elder girl's wedding?'

'Thank goodness that's all right; that's something we can take comfort from.'

'Don't let your mind wander, Leo; keep it on the problem in hand. Is this silly girl Virginia coming to her sister's wedding?'

'We don't know. We hope so. Lois doesn't think she will. I think she may. At any rate we have sent an invitation to what we hope is the right address. But even if she does come,' Chanderley made a little gesture of despair, 'What shall I say to her? Or she to me? There's a gulf between us, Theresa.'

'Of course there is. And it's very unlikely that you will be able to bridge it. If you can't make contact with the girl we have got to find somebody who can.'

'I'm all ears.'

'No good your being sarcastic, Leo. And no good your just sitting down under tribulation and accepting it, that's the Jewish blood in you; born sufferers you people, all through history. You say you don't speak the same language as the girl; well, we've got to find somebody who does speak it; somebody, to take up your rather absurd instance, who does know what a discotheque is. A man it will have to be; on the young side; attractive to women; half of him sane and knowing how to behave; half of him wild and ready for anything.'

'They grow on trees,' Chanderley said.

'They don't grow on trees, my dear Leo, but I think I can put my hand on someone who might fill the bill very adequately.'

In Soho, London amidst the strip-tease joints, the porn shops, the sleazy cinemas and the 'cheap' wine stores (adulterated plonk from Algeria dressed up as Beaune de Beau Geste and on sale at £2.15 a bottle—cost to importer 25p), more or less in the middle of all these fruits and benefits of civilisation lies Gerrard Mews, a cul-de-sac offshoot of Gerrard Street. At the end of the cul-de-sac may be found Regency House and on the first floor of that building Mr H. H. R. Hefferman, commonly known as Hooky because his too inquisitive nose had been broken a couple of times during an adventurous life, sat reading a letter.

My dear nephew,

I presume you are still engaged in that dubious *Private Investigator* business of yours. Exactly what it is that you investigate I have never known, and in any case would rather not hear about; but as it happens a friend I had not seen for many years called on me yesterday asking my advice about a personal problem and as a result I think I am able to put a commission in your way, something in which you might be able to do some good for a change. I shall expect you in Hove, therefore, on Thursday in time for dinner. It will do you good to get away for a couple of days from the rackety life that you lead in London and it will do an old woman good to see you.

Your affectionate Aunt,
Theresa Page-Foley.

P.S. when you reply do *not* put an eightpence half-penny stamp on your letter, it is quite essential not to give way more than we must to the monstrous imposition of the Post Office.

T.P-F.

Roly Watkins—caretaker of the building; confidant; incurable chatterbox and occasionally fellow conspirator—had brought the afternoon post up to his employer and stood there, frankly inquisitive, waiting to glean any information that might be forthcoming. Besides knowing the spidery Victorian handwriting he had seen the crest on the back of the envelope and so could confidently ask, 'From the old lady in Hove isn't it, Mr H.? The Honourable Mrs What-the-hell-is-the-world-coming-to?'

Hooky nodded. 'I shall be going down to visit my Aunt for a couple of days,' he said.

'Into the Valley of Death rode the six hundred,' was Roly Watkins' comment, to which he added piously, 'Gawd 'elp you; you're a better man than I am, Mr H.'

THREE

Blueprint for a job

A FEW days after the sale of pictures at Christie's the man sitting in the stalls of the Haymarket Theatre was already beginning to fear that it was going to turn out a pretty duff evening. The play had not yet come to life, nor did it look like doing so, and the girl he had been silly enough to bring along to it didn't give promise of being any more exciting either. Len couldn't think why he had lumbered himself with the silly twit. For one thing she talked too much. Chatter chatter chatter like a bloody magpie. He cut into one of her long whispered accounts of something or other to ask, 'You ever kept a magpie?'

She was startled and astonished; but at least the verbal dribble dried up. 'A magpie?'

'Oh forget it. And put a sock in it. I want to hear the play. It doesn't look like being any good but I want to hear it, so belt up.'

'Here she comes now,' said one of the characters on stage, and pat on cue, through the French windows almost obligatory in this type of faded comedy came a fresh performer evidently cognisant of

what had already been discussed and in something of a tizz about it. *'Of course if you really think the matter can be settled—'* she led off...

Len Carron wasn't particularly interested in what she was saying; he was interested in her. He had seen her before. Stanmere Gardens. As he was on his way from Roddy Marten's flat. She had obviously been going in. Roddy Marten's bit of nonsense therefore. Might be useful. And anyway, she didn't look like a bit of nonsense, she looked somehow as though she had guts. He remembered a glance of interest flashing between them on the cold stone staircase of the flats.

He consulted his programme. Virginia Cave. The name meant nothing to him, he enjoyed going to the theatre but he knew nothing about theatre people or theatre gossip.

In the first interval his companion said brightly, 'Marvellous isn't it?'

'It's a load of crap,' Len told her. 'I don't know how they've got the nerve to put it on and charge three quid a seat for looking at it.'

After the final curtain, when the thin applause had died away and God had been hurriedly, and not very musically, invited to save the Queen, Len had made up his mind. One of his firmest principles in life was never to go on struggling down the wrong road. If you find yourself lumbered with a disaster get rid of it was his motto.

He produced a five pound note.

'Here's a fiver,' he said. 'That will pay for the cab back to your place.'

She took the proffered note automatically and stared at him. 'What about you?' she asked.

'I'm going backstage to see someone.'

'Somebody in the play? Which one, Len?'

'Mind your own bloody business.'

'And what about me?'

'Another time, chick; some other time. I'm not in the mood tonight.'

'But—'

'Listen, pay for your cab; buy yourself a drink; curl up in front of the gas-fire and stupefy your bird-like brain looking at whatever nonsense there is on the box. Only I won't be there. Get it?'

Back stage was unfamiliar territory to Len Carron; the bareness of it disappointed him, he had expected something much more lush and luxurious.

A young man wearing an open-necked shirt and revealingly tight jeans directed him. 'Ginny Cave? The last door down on the right.'

Carron nodded ungraciously; he disliked homosexuals. 'Bloody pouf,' he muttered under his breath.

CARRON TOOK her out to supper at Homer's, which was well-patronised but not crowded.

'Get me a corner table,' he demanded.

'Anything you say, Mr Carron.'

'Away from the noise of that bloody machine.'

'I'll turn it down for you, Mr Carron.'

When they were settled he said, 'I enjoyed your bit.' It was only half true, but God dammit, he thought, women are women and he had a hunch that this one might be useful to him.

'I wasn't very good I'm afraid,' Virginia said. 'I made a hash of my first entrance. I always do somehow. *Of course if you really think the matter can be settled* I said, and it ought to be *arranged; of course if you really think the matter can be arranged—'*

'Does it matter?'

'Not in one way, no. But it puts you off your stroke. You know you've made a boob and half your mind is fussing about that when it all ought to be on what you're doing. What did you think of the play anyway?'

'Codswallop.'

Virginia gave a short laugh. 'Do you always say what you think, straight out, just like that?'

'Most of the time, most of the time.'

'Well, everyone seems to think the same. It's coming off at the end of the week. The notices went up tonight.'

'So you'll be out of work?'

'Half the acting profession always is.'

'Looking for a job?

The tone of his voice caught her interest.

'Why? Are you offering me one?'

Len disregarded that for the moment; he had a habit of answering questions only when it suited him.

'Are you Roddy Marten's girl?' he asked.

'I'm living with him at the moment.'

'Are you sold on him?'

'Maybe not entirely.'

'What's wrong with him?'

'He's not militant enough for me.'

Carron smiled in slight surprise. 'Are you a militant then?' he enquired.

'I'd like to pull it all down; all the established things; the Church, Parliament, the lot. It's all rotten.'

Carron laughed easily and with genuine amusement. 'Too bloody wholesale for me,' he said. 'I'm no revolutionary. I'm just a plain crook. I'm a villain. I don't want to go to the trouble of pulling everything down. I don't see the point in doing it either. I just want to fiddle my way round things, get what I can out of them. How did you get the way you are? Did you have a deprived childhood or something?'

'My real name is Chanderley. Sir Leo Chanderley is my father.'

'Is he indeed? I wouldn't say you had been deprived of much then. Didn't I see something in the papers about a wedding coming off in the family?'

Before Virginia could answer Carron had signalled to the waiter.

'Take these god-damned kidneys back and ram them down the chef's throat,' he said. 'I'm not good at eating shoe-leather. Bring me some plain cold beef instead. Rare and cut thin.'

'Very good Mr Carron. I'm sorry about the kidneys.'

'Rare and cut thin,' Carron repeated. When the waiter had gone he picked up his conversation with Virginia.

'Not your wedding by any chance is it?'

'No. My sister's.'

'I imagine it will be quite a do will it?'

'I suppose so.'

Carron eyed her with amusement. 'You going?' he asked, 'or won't your revolutionary principles let you.'

Virginia shrugged her thin shoulders. 'I might go. Not that I believe in marriage or any nonsense like that: but I might go; in fact I probably will.'

'Maybe there'll be something among the presents you could knock off for us.'

'Is that the job you were talking about?'

'No. Not my line. Can't see the point in it. I don't want to be lumbered with gold watches or silver candlesticks or diamond ear-rings. If you land yourself with that sort of gear you put yourself in the hands of the man you take it to. You've pretty well got to accept what the fence gives you. And believe me his cut isn't a small one. I don't go for stuff that's got to be changed into cash, I go for the cash itself. Can you drive?'

'Yes, of course I can.'

'Got a car?'

'No, I haven't. Not at the moment.'

'Well, never mind; that can be arranged.'

Virginia lit a cigarette, blew a cloud of smoke into the already thick atmosphere and leant back her eyes sparkling with excitement. 'God, how marvellous,' she said, 'are you really asking me to take part in a raid of some sort? I'd simply love to.'

'Don't race your motor,' Carron told her. 'Take it easy. We'll get together with Roddy and the three of us will talk it over. Maybe something can be fixed up; maybe not.'

When they finally said 'goodnight' Carron put her into a taxi outside Homer's and leant forward into the cab to give a parting word of advice. 'Remember the three wise monkeys—see nothing, hear nothing, say nothing.'

'Of course I shan't say anything to anybody, I'm much too excited about it. I shan't say a word.'

'I wouldn't if I were you. It wouldn't pay you. I don't like blabbermouths. And, listen, no need to tell Roddy Marten we've been out together this evening. Leave that to me. I'll tell him all about it at the right time. O.K.?'

'O.K. Len.'

He looked at her and laughed. 'I think you and I could get along all right,' he said. 'Leave this to me.'

IN FLAT 6 Roddy Marten poured himself out another generous gin and only faintly diluted it with water. Len Carron, who drank very little himself, watched a shade contemptuously... O.K. I suppose if the guy wants to get sozzled, he thought; there were times when he regretted having teamed up with Roddy... still, it need only be for one job and he could make that go the way he wanted... and getting to know the girl was already a bonus; he smiled slightly as he watched the other man swilling down his gin.

'What about this idea of yours, then?' Roddy asked in a sudden business-like burst. 'Got anything fixed up?'

'Yes, I have. I've got something worked out in my mind. A peach of an idea really. But there'll have to be three of us. We shall need a driver.'

'I can drive.'

'But you can't be in two places at once, can you? Even you aren't as bloody clever as that.'

'Well, you can get somebody to drive can't you?'

'I daresay I can. But the more people we get in from outside the more people who want a cut. And the more risk there is. We want somebody who's in the circle already, as it were. What about the girl I saw coming out of the flat the other day?'

'Virginia? She'd blow the whole place up if she got half a chance.'

'She won't get the chance from me. I don't want any blowing up. I want the cash handed over; no trouble, no fireworks; just the cash nice and safe and secure. Can she drive a car?'

'I suppose so. She must have had cars at home. Her father's loaded. Sir Leo Chanderley.'

'Well, she'll do then, won't she?'

'I suppose she might.'

Roddy took a fortifying sip at his glass and then set it down carefully on a side table.

'There's just one thing, Len,' he said. 'If Virginia comes in it's on the business side only. Nothing else. No funny stuff.'

Carron had difficulty in suppressing his laughter; he flattered himself that if he felt like taking Roddy Marten's girl he could do it any time he wanted.

'What are you worrying about, for Chrissake?' he asked heartily. 'I'm in this for the cash, nothing else. When's she coming back?'

'Ought to be in any minute now,' Roddy said, glancing at the clock. Len knew very well that Virginia was likely to come in at any minute since, unknown to Roddy, the two of them had lunched together.

'Give me half an hour to pave the way,' Len had said, 'and you come in about six, say; knowing nothing about anything, of course.'

The girl laughed; she was already absurdly excited over what she saw as an enjoyable escapade.

'Don't worry, Len, I'll be all dewy-eyed innocence.'

'No wonder you went on the stage.'

When Virginia appeared just after six Roddy introduced them.

'Len Carron, and this is Virginia. Virginia and I are shacked up together.'

'More or less,' Virginia said.

'And she's in a play—'

'Was. It folded three nights ago.'

'Bad luck,' Len said solemnly. 'It's nice to know you anyway. We're looking for a bit of extra talent.'

'What sort of talent?'

'Mix me a drink before we start talking,' Roddy said holding out his glass.

Passing in front of Carron on her way to the side table where the bottles were Virginia managed a wink of amused conspiracy as she went by.

'You put away a hell of a lot of that stuff,' Carron said.

'Any objection?'

'Just as long as you keep off it when we're doing the job.'

'Let's hear about this wonderful job of yours, then.'

Having handed Roddy his glass Virginia settled herself on a scruffy looking hassock.

'You all right on that thing?' Len asked.

'Of course she's all right on it,' Roddy said. 'She always sits on it, don't you, Virginia?'

'Sometimes. Yes, I'm O.K. Len, thanks.'

'Off we go then,' Carron said. 'You play poker, Roddy?'

'Poker? No. What's that got to do with anything?'

'Ah, I used to play a lot. Still do for that matter. I like poker. The point is, it isn't all luck. You want some luck, agreed. But you want some psychology as well. You've got to figure out how the other fellow's mind works. You've got to guess what he's thinking and out-think him. You've got to be just that little bit smarter. And then again you've got to pick the people you play with. I never play against the real thickheaded, wooden-witted sort. You don't win much off him. He knows what a five pound note is. And he'll never bluff. If he hasn't got the stuff he won't bet. If you're betting he chickens out straight away. If you pick up four aces you'll win the hand, sure enough; but there's no fun in it, he's never out on a limb. The chap I like to play against is the one who thinks he's clever; the one who reckons he's smart. He's apt to be so busy laughing at his own brightness that he doesn't notice you've outsmarted him. He's out on the limb and he doesn't realise you've got a saw.

'It's just the same in this wage-snatching business. There's a hell of a lot of money moved every Friday from banks all over the country to factories to pay the wages bill. By the time 4 p.m. on Friday comes round everyone has done their forty hours, or whatever it is, of fiddling, scrounging, knocking ott tor tea and attending union protest meetings and they want to be paid for their honest week's work. Good luck to 'em all, I say. Which means that the boss has to arrange for money to be transported from the bank every week. Crazy when you come to think of it isn't it? Suppose a factory has got a wage bill of a hundred thousand quid every week that means that every week one hundred thousand pieces of paper are carefully counted out, bundled up, and shunted from the strong room in the local bank to the cashier's office in the factory. Then they are bundled up again into God knows how many different pay packets and dished out to the sons of toil who can't wait to get their hands on the stuff. That's Friday afternoon; what with the supermarkets, the dogs, the betting shops and the pubs at least eight out of ten of all those pieces of paper have gone through the various tills, and have been solemnly carried back to the bank by the following Tuesday to be stashed away again in the strong room they came from. Like I say there must be something crazy about the system somewhere. If only I'd gone to college and read economics I might think up a better one.

'Still, there you are, that's the system; that's how things are done. And thank God for it. It gives honest villains like me a sporting chance.

'As far as the factory bosses go the risk is obvious and therefore according to them the remedy is obvious. You've got to get a lot of money through the streets from bank to factory so you must protect it. Villains have started using pick-axe handles and shotguns so you need heavy stuff to withstand them. It's the arms race all over again—I've got a shell which will pierce eight inches of armour plate; that's no good chum, I'm putting ten inches of plating round my next lot and so on.'

Roddy held out his glass for replenishment. 'Are we having a university extension lecture, or what?' he asked.

'Shut up Roddy,' Virginia said, 'it's fascinating.'

Carron made no comment on the sarcasm in Roddy's interruption, but he stored it in his mind; he went on as though he hadn't heard it. 'So the right way to play the hand, as I see it, is to leave the really big stakes alone. You need a pitched battle to do any good there, these days. What I'm looking for is the chap who thinks he is smart and then find a way to outsmart him and I reckon I've found one.

'There's a firm in Cricklewood called Eiger Brothers. Run by a character called Marc Eiger; whether he has got any brothers or not I wouldn't know; but he has built up a very useful little business for himself. Not in the top league, of course; nothing huge. You won't find Eiger Bros in any list of important firms; but not to worry, they are doing very nicely, thank you. Ladders, they make. Expanding ladders; patent fold-up and store away ladders; ladders for all sorts of queer jobs, and you wouldn't believe how many of the things they sell. Who the hell wants all these ladders anyway? I've never bought a ladder in my life. Still, *somebody* wants them obviously, and the result is that every week Mr Eiger pays out somewhere between fifteen and eighteen thousand pounds to the assorted collection of union officials, shop stewards and scroungers on his wages sheet.

'Now this is where the poker playing comes in. If this Eiger character was an Englishman he would play it straight—*I'm taking the lot of money through the streets,* he would say, *therefore I want protection; therefore I shall either go to the police or to some firm that specialises in protection; I'm a law-abiding citizen and I don't propose to be molested.* Fine, fine, fine. Splendid sentiments, and, in the end, probably the best thing to do. Only Marc Eiger *isn't* an Englishman; he reckons the English are pretty thick all told, else how could he have come from somewhere in Mittel Europe with nothing but the suit of clothes he was wearing (and that not paid for) and in fifteen years be the head of Eiger Bros selling ladders to everybody? He reckons the English are stupid, and all you need to outwit them is a bit of continental cunning. A bit of finesse. So what does he do? Every week the wages have to be brought from the bank to the factory. Fifteen, sixteen thousand quid. Eiger hires a Security van to make the run. Absolutely dependable firm. Two hefty fellows armed with pick-axe handles and wearing crash helmets. Heavy iron grille over the cab windows and all the rest of it. If you are going to ambush them successfully you want maybe a team of six, prepared for real rough stuff including shooting. *And even if they pulled the hold-up off they wouldn't get anything—'*

'Why not?'

'Because they would be stupid Englishmen and Marc Eiger has been too clever for them. Just after ten every Friday the Security van calls at the bank and half a dozen boxes are loaded into it. Only there's nothing in the boxes.'

'Nothing in them?'

'Not a sausage. At the same time as the van is being loaded up in front Marc Eiger's own private car—a black saloon—is in the director's car park at the back having the cash stowed away in the boot. Off goes the Security van; if any villains have made plans to attack it Eiger couldn't care less. Whilst they are busy scrapping like mad for some empty boxes his own private car, mixing with the ordinary traffic, has gone round another way and the money is safely inside the firm's premises.'

Virginia, her eyes sparkling with excitement, said, 'What a good idea.'

'It *is* a good idea,' Carron agreed. 'If a Security van runs between one bank and the factory ninety-nine per cent of people will automatically assume the wages must be in it.'

'And how do you know they are not?' Roddy asked.

'From information received,' Carron answered with a grin, 'that's the standard phrase the law uses isn't it? Cunning lot, the law; they get lots of "information received"; well, I've got a bit this time, the bit I've just told you about.'

'So what's the plan?'

'The Security van goes through all the motions properly; drives along the High Street, then takes the obvious way out to the factory and turns in through the main gates of the place. Then the gates are shut behind it. That's all part of the bluff, to convince any villains casing the job that the Security van business is genuine. Meanwhile, five minutes later, Eiger drives out of the bank car park, slips into the traffic stream and ultimately ends up in the side entrance to his works, laughing his head off, no doubt at the ease with which the stupid English can be hoodwinked. Here, give me a bit of paper, Virginia—'

The girl crossed to a hideously untidy desk in the corner by the window and came back with a writing pad in her hand. 'This O.K. Len?'

'Just what I wanted. Good girl,' he smiled at her.

Roddy looked on a trifle sourly but said nothing.

Carron produced an expensive looking ball-point pen from his pocket and drew a quick sketch.

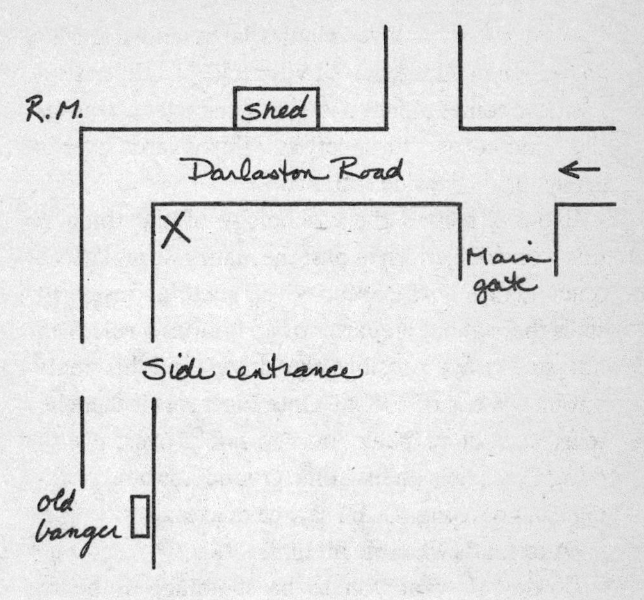

'It's a bit rough,' he said, 'but it's good enough. It's got everything in it that matters. First good point, there's very little traffic along Darlaston Road; it comes to a blind corner at one end, as you can see from the sketch; I've marked it with a cross; and then it peters out into practically nothing—a bit of waste ground and scrubby bushes and so on.

'Right; half past ten as near as makes no matter the Security van comes along where I've put an arrow and turns into the main gate of the factory. The dummy run completed once more and everyone very pleased about it. Five minutes later, and it hasn't varied much all the times I've checked it, Eiger's saloon car comes along, passes the main gate, reaches the blind corner, turns left and thirty yards later is safely inside the side entrance.

'Now, I reckon the psychology of the thing is this—once Eiger drives past the main gate and gets a quick glance at the Security van standing inside (it stays there about a quarter of an hour as a rule, I'm not sure why; possibly the driver and his mate scrounge a cup of coffee). Once Eiger sees it there he relaxes, another bank journey safely over; everything O.K.; he's on his home ground now and nothing can go wrong. Like I say, he relaxes.

'And that's when we hit him.

'Roddy, I want you to be standing, or better kneeling because you must take damned care not to be seen, just at the blind corner where I've written your initials in. I'm going to be where the road runs out into waste ground in an old banger I've got hold of. All you've got to do is to keep a lookout along Darlaston Road. You'll see the Security van turn into the main gate; keep on looking, and in five minutes, less possibly, you'll see Eiger's black saloon come along; when that's opposite the main gate you give me the signal. I'll be watching you like a hawk, don't worry.

'I then drive my old wreck up the side road—on the wrong side of the road of course—and crash into Eiger just as he is coming round the blind corner. He won't be going fast, it's a right angle turn, and I shall be only just moving. But there'll be a bit of a crunch, of course, radiator stoved in and bodywork dented and so on, and whilst Eiger is still worrying about his lovely saloon car you and I scare him to death with a dummy gun, bundle him out, tie him up and sellotape his mouth. I reckon the two of us can manage that in about three minutes flat, don't you?'

'Easy.'

'And what about me?' Virginia asked.

'Don't worry, your turn's coming; the whole thing depends on you doing your bit O.K. See where I've marked SHED on the plan? O.K. there *is* an old shed there, disused now; it's open to the road and it goes back quite a good way. You'll be driving my car, Virginia, a Ford Cortina—you can manage that?'

'Perfectly, I used to drive one regularly.'

'Good. Right, you'll be sitting in the Cortina at the back of the shed with the engine switched off. You'll hear the crash, of course, and when you do, switch on, drive the Cortina out of the shed into Darlaston Road and open up the boot. As soon as Roddy and I have trussed up smart-Alec Eiger we'll get the bags of notes out of his car and bring them up to the Cortina. You keep the engine running and the moment the last bundle is in off we go—at least fifteen thousand quid to the good.'

Virginia laughed excitedly. 'What a perfectly marvellous idea Len,' she cried. 'When shall we do it?'

'Before long,' Carron said, smiling back at her. 'In a few days. I'll let you know. I'll be seeing you again soon, don't worry.'

FOUR

Ph.D.

'THURSDAY IN time for dinner' the ukase had been worded, and Hooky was not likely to disobey it. The chunky six-footer was not a man noticeably indoctrinated with respect for rules and regulations but there were certain basic facts, such as the law of gravity, the ultimate onset of death and any pronouncement made by his Aunt Theresa which he had the sense to recognise as inevitable. It was foolish to try to evade them. It was easier to comply.

But compliance need not entail abject surrender. 'Dinner' meant eight o'clock. As far as Theresa Page-Foley was concerned that was the law of the Medes and Persians; for her it always had been eight in the days of the green-baize door, Venables the butler supervising matters in the dining-room and a footman behind every chair; and for her it always would be eight.

'In time for dinner' could therefore be reasonably interpreted as seven-thirty, or even stretching a point, seven forty-five. A man who had had the sense to arrive in Hove shortly after six could reckon on at least an hour which might be profitably employed.

Hooky was employing his hour in the most profitable way that he knew; he was in the Wheatsheaf talking to Mrs Drew.

Hooky, a connoisseur of pubs, had discovered the Wheatsheaf by accident on a previous visit to Hove. Just when he had been coming to the dismal conclusion that the real, genuine, dyed-in-the-wool, soul saving article simply did not exist among the genteel boarding-houses and the fatuous little bridge clubs that cluttered up the landscape he had turned a corner, glanced casually down what was little more than an alleyway, the remnant of a once thriving mews, and there he saw the noble sign swinging easily in the wind.

The sign looked right somehow.

Hooky explored, pushed his way in and knew at once that the sign had not lied; the inside of the Wheatsheaf was right too. It had everything—decency, restraint, and the reverential hush proper to the consideration of serious matters; propped up against the bar was a gentleman in a smart cloth cap obviously intent on doing his liver no good at all and only too ready, if you wanted to know it, to tell you the story of his life; and behind the bar was Mrs Drew.

For *was* read *reigned.*

Behind the bar, then, reigned Mrs Drew. Mrs Drew had the attributes of regality. She looked like a gipsy queen, a gipsy queen whose dark eyes could suddenly flash with unexpected and excited fire; she had a splendid bosom, a veritable platform of impregnable, and yet at the same time provocative, propriety; above her finely chiselled face a mass of raven black hair was built up in a fantastic superstructure of remarkable design. Every one of her regulars would enthusiastically have gone to bed with her; not one of them, not even Hooky, had ever dared to suggest it.

When Hooky came in she recognised him at once; but, then, that soldier of fortune had the knack of impressing himself on women's consciousness. She greeted him by name and Hooky felt suitably flattered, reflecting that it was all of three months since she had last seen him.

'I couldn't come to Hove,' he declared, 'and not look in on the Wheatsheaf.'

The imposing head was inclined in recognition of the compliment. 'I expect you'll find it much the same as ever,' Mrs Drew said, 'things don't alter much.'

Looking round Hooky came to the conclusion, with profound gratitude for at least one small island of stability in a shifting world, that things didn't seem to have altered at all: a bright fire made nonsense of the cold of an April evening; every particle of brasswork gleamed; Mrs Drew, of course, was Mrs Drew; there was even a Cloth Cap there in the proper place.

'I was about to order a replenishment of my glass,' Cloth Cap said. 'May I ask you to join me, sir?'

Hooky begged, as the newcomer, to be allowed to do the honours, and Cloth Cap acceded gracefully. 'Mrs Drew knows what's good for me,' he said.

Hooky watched with some dismay whilst first a double brandy was poured out and then a shot of vodka added to it.

'I don't know whether it's good for you Doctor Crawley,' Mrs Drew said severely, 'but it's what you like.'

'Apt to be very strict with me the good dame is,' Cloth Cap said, eyeing his lethal drink with the gleeful anticipation of the true addict. 'And incidentally it's Stuart-Crawley with a hyphen. Mrs Drew doesn't believe in hyphens. And when I say *doctor* I am not talking about the ills of the body many of which are illusory anyway and most of which can be cured by judicious application of this admirable mixture'—he held up his glass and regarded it in reverential fashion—'no sir, Philosophy.'

'You are a Doctor of Philosophy?' Hooky asked.

'I am, sir. Ph. bloody D. For what it's worth. Which incidentally is a very great deal. Thought is the structure of the Universe. Did you know that, sir? I'm afraid I didn't catch your name—'

'Hefferman. Commonly known as Hooky. For obvious reasons. Do you often drink brandy and vodka mixed?'

'As often as I can meet a man civilised and generous enough to provide it. Your nose was broken in contact with life, I take it?'

Hooky laughed. 'That's a very fair description of what happened,' he allowed. 'I've been a shade too inquisitive, too often, in too many places.'

'It somehow suits you Mr Hefferman,' Mrs Drew said. 'I like a man that looks as though he has really been a man.'

'That's a side-swipe at me,' the Ph.D. explained. 'Fill my glass again, Mrs D., would you please? Explaining my philosophy of life to minds ill-attuned to comprehend it I find tiring work. Thirsty work. You'll have another Pimms, sir, won't you?'

Hooky had only just started on his first Pimms, but he polished it off like a man and stood in the queue; he could see it was going to be one of those evenings, this philosophic bird seemed to have swallowed a sponge or something...

'Yes, sir, a side-swipe at me. And a justified one. As usual Mrs D. is right. I haven't lived. I have existed, mesmerised into inaction by an unmeaning miasma of nonsensical speculation. That sentence is a shade too alliterative. I was always warning the little sods, excuse me I should perhaps say my pupils, against the dangers of alliteration. Too facile, too easy. *Facilis descensus est Averno.* Don't be alarmed, Mrs D., that isn't anything rude—'

'One can never be sure with you, doctor; I never know what little game you are up to.'

'That's one of the many things the actress said to the bishop,' Dr Stuart-Crawley continued. 'Latin, Mrs D., the universal language. Just as love is the universal passion, God help us.'

'I take it you are a schoolmaster?' Hooky ventured.

'A hack, sir. A decayed tutor. A dominie. Devoting my life to the profitless and impossible task of introducing civilised ideas into the thick heads of dedicated barbarians. English I endeavour to teach the little brats, and art. May God who called forth Michelangelo, Rubens and van Gogh out of the slime of the earth forgive me.'

'You are an artist yourself perhaps?'

'An art critic, sir. Those who can, do; those who can't, teach; those who aren't any good at doing and not much good at teaching take up as a side line telling others where they have gone wrong.'

'And where did you go to school, Mr Hefferman?' Mrs Drew enquired.

'I was educated at home,' Hooky said, 'and in my spare time I went to Eton.'

'A witticism,' the doctor explained. 'God help us, a witticism; but I like it. And a witticism on two Pimms. For two Pimms I'll crack a joke. I'm sorry. I apologise. Occasionally puerilities like that rise to my lips. It comes of consorting with the boys. Consort is only too right, unfortunately. No doubt you remember the delicate Arabian couplet—

there is a boy across the river with a bottom
like a peach
alas, I cannot swim.

The whole tragedy of the human situation is there; apprehension of beauty; desire; frustration; resignation. I am ready for another of my refreshing draughts, if you are prepared to pay for it.'

Hooky reached for his wallet somewhat apprehensively; this English-and-Art-combined bird was undoubtedly amusing but equally he was undoubtedly expensive.

'Are you sure all this brandy is good for you doctor?' Mrs Drew asked.

'No, I am not sure of it, my dear Mrs D. I am sure of nothing. I move uncertainly through the misty landscape of doubt. You remember, of course, the opening sentence in the Metaphysics of Aristotle—*all men desire by nature to know.* It may well be true;

the old Greek pederast—good luck to him—may have hit the nail on the head; but between desiring to know and certainty a great gulf is fixed. You recognise the biblical allusion, sir? I am a great reader of the bible, and indeed of other works of fiction. A great gulf is fixed, I say, and in the alarming bewilderment of that gulf, floundering as it were in an unthreadable maze, I find this'—he held up his glass—'a comfort and a stay. May I ask what profession you follow, sir?'

You may ask, Hooky thought, and since he was finding the conversation amusing he made answer.

'I profit from the idiocies of mankind. I am a Private Investigator. I make my living investigating the crimes and follies of the world.'

'Then, by God sir, you must be a millionaire.'

'The last time you were in,' Mrs Drew said, 'you were going to see your Aunt I remember.'

'I have been summoned to the dread presence again,' Hooky told her; glancing up at the clock above the bar he added, 'And I mustn't be late.'

'You look apprehensive, sir,' Doctor Stuart-Crawley said.

'I *am* apprehensive,' Hooky admitted. 'My Aunt is an apprehension inducer.'

'I don't blame you,' the doctor said. 'Aunts are by nature formidable creatures. I once had an Aunt who composed Latin hexameters in her cold bath every morning and who ate grass.'

Hooky said his Aunt would eat him if he was late for dinner.

'Ah, if you are dining with an Aunt of that quality, sir, you need sustenace—Mrs D. . . .'

Hooky managed to escape about seven twenty and he stood for a moment or two in the now dark alleyway outside the Wheatsheaf extremely glad of the cool evening air. The double brandy and vodka merchant had seemed genuinely sorry to be left on his own and he was evidently settling down to play a long innings. Hooky, who in his time had drunk hard in many of the famous bars up and down the world, rated the doctor high amongst all the performers he had known. Definitely an alpha-plus man.

In the flat he was greeted by Mrs Page-Foley in one of her most amiable moods.

'You've come in good time,' she complimented him. 'I approve of that. I dislike unpunctuality. And I suppose you have brought your usual bad habits with you; you will find the drinks set out on the little French table in the corner. Please be careful not to spill anything on the table top, it's valuable.'

Hooky said that one way and another he didn't think he would bother about a drink, thank you very much.

His Aunt looked at him suspiciously. 'Are you all right?' she demanded.

Hooky said that he was perfectly all right but that he seemed to have gone off drink just lately somehow.

'I didn't know you had so much sense,' the old lady commented. 'It gives me hope of getting a sensible answer to what I want to talk to you about—' the French ormolu clock over the fireplace struck eight tinkling notes. 'But dinner first,' she added, 'and you must excuse any shortcomings in a meal I have had to prepare myself, although in my opinion I manage just as well as any cook I ever had to pay wages to.'

Over after-dinner coffee she opened the proceedings by saying, 'You will shortly be getting an invitation to a wedding—'

Hooky shot a quick glance at the indomitable old figure, sitting in the uncompromising bolt upright posture which she had been taught in the nursery and had never forgotten or relaxed. A wedding? Was it possible? Was he to be given news of an autumnal, indeed a winter, flowering of romance? Had some brave man really been foolhardy enough?

'Well, that's good news,' he ventured cautiously.

'Is it?' Mrs Page-Foley snapped, 'I'm not so sure. A great number of weddings nowadays seem to me to be acts of pure folly, embarked upon with a total disregard for what will be the inevitable outcome. Incidentally you ought to get married yourself, Hooky. You should look out for a nice sensible girl—'

'I keep looking out,' Hooky said in his defence, 'but unfortunately the sensible girls are so seldom nice.'

'In any case it's not exactly the wedding I want to talk to you about. The girl who is going to get married is Rachel Chanderley, the elder daughter of Leo Chanderley. Sir Leo Chanderley. Who isn't "Sir" or "Lord" these days? But Leo probably deserved it. He has obviously been highly successful; successful enough to have a house in Eaton Square anyway. And of course he married well. Lois. One of the Cumbridge girls. And now, as I say, one of his own girls is getting married. I suppose you have still got the proper clothes for a wedding by the way?'

'There'll always be a Moss Bros,' Hooky pointed out.

'I suppose there will. We live in a synthetic and substitute age. Rachel is the girl getting married. Leo's got Jewish ancestry behind him. And proud of it. As he has every right to be. Scratch a Jew and you find a civilised man; and, so I've been told, a very ardent lover. Rachel is marrying a naval man apparently.'

'Sailors are quite good at it too,' Hooky said, 'so Rachel ought to be O.K.'

'It isn't Rachel I want to talk about, it's the other girl, Virginia.'

'Has she got herself fixed up?'

'It seems that she has got herself into a most stupid mess. Now I know perfectly well, Hooky, that you are much better at getting girls into trouble than out of it, but I think that in this instance you might really be able to do some good.'

Mrs Page-Foley proceeded to recount the substance of what had passed between Leo Chanderley and herself whilst Hooky listened with interest and admiration. With interest for what she was telling him, and with admiration for the teller of the tale; the old girl might be knocking eighty, he thought, but nobody could be more on the ball. She had a marvellously sharp eye for human folly and a splendidly sharp tongue for giving her opinion of it; and under it all she clearly wanted to do a good turn for her old chum Sir Leo Eaton Square Chanderley...

'Well, as far as I can understand it,' Hooky said when his Aunt had finished outlining the scenario, 'I've got to do a reforming act. I might as well buy myself a tambourine and join the Salvation Army.'

'I very much doubt if they would have you. For once in a way, Hooky, you have a chance of doing something sensible, something constructive; there is a young girl, and I don't doubt she is an attractive young girl, involved; and equally I have no doubt that Leo Chanderley will act handsomely in the matter of a present or fee if you want to be coarse.'

'I can seldom resist the temptation to be coarse,' Hooky said smiling at his Aunt.

FIVE

Pieces in a jigsaw

A COMFORTABLE, secure feeling was warm inside Marc Eiger; the previous night had been agreeably uxorious, which he had enjoyed, for Bernice was plump and willing; breakfast had been just as he liked it with the coffee splendidly hot and a satisfied Bernice fussing about his every need, seeing that the toast and everything else was just right; then arrival at the office a minute or two after eight. Long before anybody else would turn up, of course; but then they were Englishmen and trades unionists, and Eiger—he thanked his own peculiar God—was neither.

As usual he spent the first ten minutes studying the *Financial Times*... 'production at British Leyland has again been halted...' he read, and reading it shook his head in sorrowful unbelief; *God Almighty,* he wondered, *why is this stupid nation so keen on cutting its own throat?*... 'South Wales miners discuss possibility of £150 weekly wage', at that he could only manage a despairing laugh *'cloud cuckoo land'* he thought *'sheer cloud cuckoo land';* the city news was more cheering; the F.T. index was still, unaccountably, over the four hundred mark and on Wall Street the Dow Jones had moved up.

He began to open the morning mail and had soon forgotten the disturbing F.T. headlines. There was no shortage of orders. The new 'Eiger Collapsible' which had got off to rather a sticky start six months ago was now getting into its stride and looked like being a real winner; plenty of troubles and worries, of course; always had been; in business always would be; but with an order book full and overflowing, it wasn't unreasonable to feel a bit satisfied with yourself...

At nine the staff came in; no absentees today he thought; trust them not to be missing today, Friday, wages day. When he next glanced at the ultra modern chromium faced clock the half hour had already gone by. He began to make preparations for his weekly visit to the bank. Every week it gave him very considerable pleasure to reflect on his own cleverness in the matter. The Security van would be there making its dummy run on scheduled time, and if there were any villains about (personally he didn't believe there would be villains in his own homely High Street) but if there were villains about and they tried any nonsense they would find themselves outwitted by the clever little business man from Mittel

Europe. He was humming contentedly to himself as he went out to his car...

Virginia sat in the driving seat of the Cortina smoking. Everything had worked out just as Len had told her it would. She had come along Darlaston Road past the factory gate and there the shed was, open to the road and roomy. She had had no difficulty in getting tucked away inconspicuously in position. If she strained to one side she could just see the bit of roadway in front of Eiger Brothers' gate. She kept an eye on the dashboard clock...coming up to 10.25...when she took the cigarette from her lips to flick off the ash her hand shook a little; she didn't mind that, in fact she rather welcomed it; she was excited and she was enjoying being excited... *Christ, this is fun* she said to herself; her mind went back to the evening at Homer's; her first evening out with Len; *codswallop* he had called the play; she laughed again, remembering; you knew where you were with Len, that was what she liked about him...and *I think you and I could get along all right* he had said. She thought so, too; she thought she and Len Carron could get along together very well. Len was the sort of man you caught fire with...10.29 on the clock; she wound down the window and threw away her half smoked cigarette, she was leaning right over to one side now, her eyes glued on the road...10.31, 2, on the clock...Len said they were always on time and Len knew; she was convinced of that; Len had got this thing worked out and wrapped up and it was marvellously exciting working with him...10.34 and there it was! The Security van. Unmistakable. Exactly as Len had said it would be. It turned into the works entrance and disappeared from her sight...any minute now she thought; she wasn't in any way scared or nervous, just tremendously excited; high on excitement...

THE TWO middle-aged ladies in the saloon car in the High Street were bickering. This was no unusual circumstance, they lived together, were in one another's close company for about sixteen hours out of every twenty-four, bickered for most of those sixteen hours and were firm and indissoluble friends.

'Ethel, why didn't you bring the map?'

'I thought I had brought it, Connie.'

'But you *haven't* brought it, my dear, have you?'

'You can't read a map anyway. Don't you remember when we tried to go to Horsham that Sunday and you read the map wrong and we ended up completely lost.'

'You never forget that, do you? Of course I can read a map; only, thanks to your forgetfulness, I haven't got a map to read.'

'Let's ask this man with the dog. I think men with dogs are always dependable, don't you? Do you remember how old Jacob loved the car.'

'Of course I remember how old Jacob loved the car. What a silly thing to ask...'

Surprisingly the man with the dog was not a stranger in those parts, nor was he semi-literate; he was knowledgeable and helpful.

'Heatherdene? Well, yes, now let me see...go over the traffic lights just ahead of you, and right on to the end of the High Street. There's a roundabout there. You've got to go round it of course; and as you are going round it take the—now, let me see, take the third, or is it the second, no third I think, turn on your left and that's the road you want.'

The ladies were suitably grateful.

As they drove on Ethel said, 'I knew a man with a dog would be able to help us. What sort of dog was that, Connie?'

'A Basenji.'

''A Basenji? I honestly don't think it was a Basenji.'

'Of course it was a Basenji. Didn't you see the way its tail curled?'

'Lots of dogs have curly tails.'

'Not like that.'

'I thought it was some sort of husky.'

'Really, my dear Ethel! Haven't you ever been to Crufts?'

'Of course I've been to Crufts. We went together in 1975.'

'1974.'

'I'm quite sure it was '75, because if you remember—'

'Is this the roundabout he was talking about do you suppose?'

'It must be. He said the traffic lights first and then the roundabout.'

'I hate roundabouts.'

'It's quite simple—'

'It's perfectly simple if you aren't driving. Which turn off did he say to take?'

'Did he say the second or third?'

'Good God, Ethel, I'm asking you. Look at this huge great thing coming from the right—'

'Let it go for heavens sake.'

'Of course I'm going to let it go. Really one would think you had never driven with me before. The second on the left did that man say?'

'It was either second or third—'

'Well, anyway we've taken the second.'

'I expect it will be all right. We must be going in the right general direction anyway.'

'You're so vague. That's always been your trouble, of course. There's a name up, did you catch it?'

'Darlaston Road. Do you think that's right?'
'We should know if you had brought the map.'

WHERE DARLASTON ROAD ceased to be a road and petered out into waste ground with a few scrubby bushes making a dusty effort at survival Len Carron stood by the side of the old banger smoking.

He was ready, if anybody should come along, to pretend he was carrying out an adjustment to the windscreen wiper. Not that he thought it likely that anyone would come along; he had done his homework pretty thoroughly, had Len, and one reason why Eiger Bros made such an attractive target was that the works were so isolated. Unless you were actually heading for the Eiger works there was no reason for coming along Darlaston Road. Len could imagine that at night time courting couples might find the waste ground in which the road lost itself attractive; but this wasn't night time; it was half past ten in the morning. Action time. If he lifted his head he could see Roddy Marten crouching behind the bit of straggling hedge that still grew at the corner; although he couldn't see her he knew that the girl was all set in his own Cortina in the shed... His taut, scarred face relaxed in a momentary smile when he thought of Virginia; he remembered catching sight of her for the first time outside Marten's flat... *that one's got something* he had thought, *there's some-*

thing about her; she was too good for Roddy Marten, anyway, and it might be fun persuading her that she was, provided that she dropped all this pull-down-and-smash-up-the-lot business; that was just plain bloody daft and if they were to get on together she would have to be told so.

Time was getting on and now he kept his eye fixed permanently on Roddy Marten... *when you see the car following the Security van just lift your hand, that's all; and when you hear the crash out you come running like the clappers and we'll truss this Eiger bugger up properly*... sixteen thousand nicker or thereabouts, Len ruminated; very nice too; dolce vita for a bit; with Virginia, could be; no difficulty about getting it either and all because a little smart Alec Jewboy thinks he's so much cleverer than us poor yobos...

Roddy Marten's hand went up; instantly Len went into action. He threw away his half smoked cigarette and stepped into the car. The engine came to life at once and keeping in bottom gear and grinning at the anticipation of what was going to happen he drove very slowly, on the wrong side of the road towards the blind corner...

IT WAS all timed perfectly; the front bumpers of the two cars and then their radiators met almost head on, crunch, crash... Len knew that nobody would be hurt, there wasn't enough speed on either side for that; he didn't want anybody hurt, least of all himself; he just wanted someone scared, good and proper...

He seized the dummy shot-gun from the passenger's seat, kicked open the door and jumped out. When he pulled open the door of the saloon car he was flabbergasted. For a moment he was completely non-plussed. Instead of the smart Alec Jewboy with sixteen thousand nicker ready to be picked up there were two scared-to-death elderly women with sweet-fanny-adams...

Ethel tried to say *Connie what is it?* Connie tried to ask *Ethel what's happening?* Both were too frightened to do more than croak unintelligibly.

'Who the hell are you?' Len demanded, and then catching sight of Roddy Marten who had come running up to the other side of the car he roared at him furiously, 'it's the wrong car, you bloody fool. Come on out of it.'

SIX

'It all went off splendidly'

LOIS HAD said, 'I know quite well that the world is falling apart—at any rate the world *we* know; but for once, just for this once Leo, let's pretend that it isn't. Let's do the thing properly; let's do it in style.'

Leo Chanderley willingly agreed; 'style' suited the woman he was married to. He had discussed with her his visit to Hove—'Theresa Page-Foley, a remarkable old character,' he explained.

'An old flame of yours?' Lois teased.

'At any rate, we knew one another in the old days, I'll say that much. I don't know how old she is now, but really she's one of these ageless people.'

'And this nephew of hers?'

'Well, Theresa is no fool. Of all people she is the most *un*foolish. She suggested this chap Hefferman. Hooky they call him apparently; and if she says she thinks he can help he very probably can; I'm willing to believe her. I'm willing to give it a try; especially now that I've seen him and had a talk. I like the look of him, I like the feel of him. And after all he is Theresa's nephew and he did go to Eton—'

Lois was amused. 'Half the scoundrels I've known in my life went to Eton,' she said.

'Hefferman isn't a scoundrel,' Leo put in quietly.

'Probably not. Let us hope not anyway. In any case he can't possibly be worse company for Ginny than the lot she seems to have taken up with, so let us invite him by all means.'

'And you think Ginny herself will come?'

'It will be the saddest thing if she doesn't—to her own sister's wedding—but, then, a mother's heart has to get used to sad things.'

So Hooky duly got his gilt-edged invitation delivered to his somewhat disreputable office in Soho... pleasure of your company...Commander Ronald St John Dellington R.N....Church of St Peter... afterwards 292 Eaton Square...R.S.V.P.... The invitation, propped up on Hooky's desk, filled Roly Watkins with curiosity.

'Eaton Square, eh? Mixing with the nobs, then, are you?'

'It will be a change from Regent Mews.'

'What's this R.S.V.P. bit? Real Snobs Very Posh, is that it?'

'Something like that. How anyone can be as steeped in sin as you are and yet remain so lamentably ignorant I really don't know.'

Roly grinned. 'That's the sort of thing your Honourable Aunt says to you, guvnor, isn't it? I hope as you won't let the side down; you'll be giving them a good present, I suppose?'

'I shall be giving them the pleasure of my company.'

'They'll enjoy that, I'm sure,' Roly said.

There were no disasters in the church, everyone turned up on time; the chief actors spoke their lines audibly and as though they meant them; and the Navy, in spite of the traditional bachelor's binge the night before, turned itself out all present and correct. *Here comes the bride* the organ blared; 'doesn't she look sweet' half the customers said (she did); 'isn't he handsome' the other half whispered (he was)...*to have and to hold from this day forward* the fine words rolled out and Lois felt a little stab at her heart remembering various things...ups and downs, of course, but on the whole it had been all right for herself and Leo; more than all right; except for Ginny, except for Ginny...

Hooky wasn't surprised to find the house in Eaton Square packed; he knew the formula—give 'em hardly enough space to breathe and a good deal too much to drink and they'll go away saying what a wonderful party it was.

'I won't introduce you,' Lois had said, 'because if I did she would probably suspect something. And, of course, she may not turn up. But if she does you won't have any difficulty in recognising her because she looks exactly like me.'

'She must be a damned good-looker then,' Hooky averred.

Lois laughed; she ran a quick appraising eye over this husky, chunky masculine creature who wore his morning clothes with an undeniable air.

'I understand you have quite a reputation with the ladies, Mr Hefferman,' she said, 'and I am quite sure you deserve it.'

Hooky grinned at her; he liked quality wherever he saw it, and this one had it.

The one with quality was quite right; there was no difficulty in recognising the daughter, nor any difficulty in deciding that she, too, showed quality after a somewhat rakish fashion. Hooky watched her across the crowded room. 'Damn it she's only a kid really,' he thought, but he remembered a little sadly that kids nowadays had a wonderful knack of getting themselves into all sorts of trouble; kids, after all, could throw brickends, and carry flick knives and smoke pot and generally contrive to break their mothers' hearts...

Virginia was on her third glass of champagne already. She didn't know whether she was glad she had come or not. In the church she had done her best to whip herself up into the proper state of contemptuous superiority...*gathered together in the sight of*

God—they were always so free with their references to this God of theirs, how many of this lot believed in him anyway?... *'till death do us part'*, at a rough guess forty per cent of the congregation were already divorced and probably a further twenty per cent actively thinking about it...*and thereto I plight thee my troth.* Never in the whole of their lives in any circumstances would either that unbearably superior sister of hers or the polished naval mannikin she was foolishly marrying ever use the word *troth* again, quite possibly they were not entirely sure what it meant—mumbo jumbo, like all religion, the opium of the people... and yet—

And yet, no good denying it, there was something about the whole affair—some of the words might be silly but some of them were rather fine; the tunes might be trumpery but hadn't somebody said something about the potency of cheap music? Rachel was unbearably superior but she undoubtedly knew how to wear a wedding dress. Virginia sipped her champagne and turned her thoughts away from the immediate scene to her own position... God Almighty what a shambles... she had thought Len was actually going to beat up Roddy Marten when they had all got together at Len's place after the farcical mess-up of their plans...

DIDN'T I TELL YOU Eiger's car was a big black saloon?

You told me Eiger's car would come immediately after the Security van, a couple of minutes or so after it; so when the van had turned into the works entrance and, like you had said, there was this saloon car a couple of minutes after it I naturally—

Naturally my arse. You never stopped to take a good look and check on things. You were so bloody fidgety and on edge you shot your hand up straight away.

RODDY MARTEN remained sullenly silent.

Virginia looked from one man to the other in fascination; she already knew which way all her inclinations were taking her; to her surprise Len suddenly burst out laughing 'Jeese, those two old trouts were scared,' he said, 'scared out of their lives, I wonder they didn't both have a heart attack.' His laughter left his voice abruptly and he turned on Roddy again. 'You know what you did, don't you?' he demanded. 'You messed the whole effing thing up. I don't reckon you're much good at this sort of thing, Marten.'

Marten stared at him for a few seconds in silence; if he had been going to say anything belligerent he thought better of it and substituted, 'Then you had better get on without me hadn't you? Come on, Virginia.'

When he reached the door and turned back to face the room Virginia was still seated; Len Carron had selected a cigarette and was engaged in lighting it, in apparent disregard of anything else that might be happening, but just before he snapped out the lighter flame he shot a quick hard look at the girl.

Virginia was aware of the look; she was aware that she was at a minor crisis in her life; she was aware that because of the way she had chosen to live there would frequently be a crisis, minor or major; she was aware that she didn't want it otherwise, it was the kind of life she enjoyed.

'I think I'll stay on and talk to Len a bit,' she said.

Roddy stared at her from the doorway. 'Does that mean you aren't coming back to the flat?' he asked at length.

'I'm going to stay on and talk to Len for a bit.'

Carron leant back, blew a smoke ring up towards the ceiling and watched its slow disintegration with the greatest attention as though nothing else in the world had the slightest interest for him. At the doorway Marten still hesitated; out of the corner of an eye Len Carron watched him, amused; *if he's bloody fool enough to play it rough* he thought *I'll have to let him have it,* but whatever momentary temptation may have been in Roddy Marten's mind he contented himself in the end with slamming the door violently and he went out onto the landing.

Len laughed. 'Good riddance,' he said. 'There's a room at the top of this block empty. A flatlet they call it. One room really. You could move in there if you wanted to. It might come in handy at times; but I warn you I'm a bit of a loner, always have been, I don't mind a bit of fun now and again but I don't want anybody cluttering me up...'

'Virginia Cave isn't it?'

The query brought Virginia back with a jolt to the immediate realities of the reception. She shot a look at the man who had come up to her. She wasn't at all certain that she liked what she saw, this one looked just a shade too damned sure of himself, she thought, as though things would always go his way and he would take it all for granted. Still she had to admit that it was nice to be recognised... *Virginia Cave* he had said and even if in your heart of hearts you knew you would never be an Ellen Terry still, you were an actress and to have a public was the breath of life to you...

'A shame that play at the Haymarket folded,' Hooky went on (he had been doing his homework).

'Did you like it?' she asked eagerly.

Not having seen the play Hooky knew he was on dangerous ground here, but he also knew, from personal experience of the comic business of life, that there was no truth whatsoever in the pompous dictum *flattery will get you nowhere;* Hooky was firmly convinced that the exact opposite was true, that judiciously applied, now with finesse, now with a trowel, flattery would go a long way towards getting you wherever you wanted to be, especially with the dear creatures who capered about on the stage and imagined they had grease-paint in their veins; 'I thought *you* were jolly good,' he said with what sounded like immense conviction.

It made pleasant hearing, but in point of fact Virginia was not altogether convinced.

'Someone came behind and said he thought it was codswallop,' she said.

'Must have been a half-wit,' Hooky pronounced firmly.

Virginia smiled slightly. 'I wouldn't call him that,' she said.

'Just a candid boyfriend of yours, maybe?' Hooky ventured.

'And what the hell have my boyfriends got to do with you?'

Hooky grinned amiably; he realised that he had a tricky bit of knitting on his hands here.

'Just masculine curiosity,' he answered her. 'Very understandable in the circumstances, with a girl as attractive as you are.'

'The next thing I am supposed to say is *I bet you say that to everyone* and then you answer *only to a girl who is intelligent as well as good looking*—isn't that how the scenario goes?'

'Along those lines,' Hooky agreed cheerfully. 'I must say it's very refreshing to come across somebody who knows her part so well; comes of being a highly professional actress I expect.'

She had to smile at that. She took a second look at this amusing extrovert—who the hell was he, anyway?

'Are you a friend of the family?' she asked.

'Not really. In a roundabout way. At one remove as you may say.'

'I'm no good at riddles. Maybe you're just a gate crasher?'

'Do I look like a gate crasher?'

'Yes, you do. Very much so.'

'I may have crashed a few gates in my time,' Hooky admitted 'but not today. I am here representing my Aunt who in her green and salad days—though it is difficult to imagine the formidable old dragon ever enjoying such a period—used to know the bride's father and mother well it appears. That was in the dim and distant. Before you were born. The aged Aunt, who lives in Hove, didn't feel equal to coming herself to this jamboree so she detailed me.' Hooky paused for a second and then added, blatantly, 'and as things have turned out how glad I am that I came along.'

'Do you always chat a girl up like that?'

'Only when she's intelli—oh Lord, we've had that bit already haven't we? Not always, no. Only when it looks worth while.'

'And do you live in Hove with this Aunt of yours?'

'That's a dreadful thing to suggest,' Hooky said. 'You shouldn't say things like that. I live in this slatternly sloven of a city, this ancient citadel of litter and licentiousness. I live in the heart—if it's got one—of Soho, where every now and again, maybe once a day, I meet a fellow Englishman and my spirit rejoices—and you?'

Virginia gave a little smile and said, 'I've moved recently.'

'You don't live here in Eaton Square?'

'I wouldn't live here for a fortune.'

'You probably couldn't live here without one.'

'I think the whole thing is a farce—the whole set-up.'

'And if you were offered a part in a farce wouldn't you accept it?'

'Don't try to be clever, please. The whole framework of society is rotten and we ought to pull it down.'

'Leave my bit standing like a good girl,' Hooky begged. 'What about a spot of dinner together one evening? I'm a lonely man.'

'Loneliness is very good for some people,' Virginia said as she moved away and mingled with the crowd of guests.

Hooky, too drifted away, making, as he went, mental assessment of the state of play so far. He had to admit that he had not exactly been a riot, but on the other hand he didn't think that he had done too badly for a beginning. The girl interested him and if he hadn't got quite as far with her as he would have wished, well, for the moment enough was enough. Softlee, softlee catchee monkey...

The room was crowded, Hooky knew a fair number of the guests if not intimately at least on the 'hail-fellow-what-news-on-the-Rialto' level. As he moved slowly through the throng he tried to keep a discreet eye on Virginia to take note of any people she palled up with particularly.

'And what are you doing at a nonsensical function like this, Mr Hefferman? I should have thought you had more sense.'

Hooky knew the curious, high-pitched voice well. Once heard never forgotten. He turned to greet the owner of it, and could only just refrain from laughing. It was difficult to assess the age of the morning clothes Julius Bern was wearing; from the antiquity of their cut and the shiny shabbiness of them they might well have belonged to his impoverished grandfather.

Friendship between the millionaire teetotal miser and the always hard-up extrovert consumer of Pimms Number One was an unlikely development. Nor did it, in fact, exist; but once in his life, and by sheer accident, Hooky had done the other man a service and to give him his due Bern had never forgotten it.

It had happened in Funchal, Madeira. On the bathing and sun-bathing slabs of Reid's. Julius Bern, who was frightened of the water anyway, had not the slightest intention of bathing and very little intention of sun-bathing either; his total concession in that regard was to take off a black alpaca jacket, and on his head to substitute what looked like his under-gardener's working straw hat for the appalling multi-coloured beret which he usually wore.

Hooky had been swimming, diving, water-skiing and generally disporting himself with enormous gusto in an Atlantic which was far from calm. He had not the slightest idea who the queerly dressed old codger hunched in a deck chair near the edge of the bathing slabs was.

Hooky's problem at the moment was a typical one for him—should he make his way up to the bar on the cliff top and order that most satisfying of post-swim drinks, a Bovril and Madeira, or stay on where he was for a while and continue to try to attract the attention of the divinely tall, long-legged Swedish girl sun-bathing not many yards away?

These two agreeable alternatives were occupying his mind when the customary peace of the bathing slabs was broken by shouts of alarm and warning.

'People screaming their heads off,' Hooky thought, 'what the hell's up? This sort of thing doesn't happen at Reid's.'

The next moment it had happened and he realised what it was. One of the freak waves (volcanic in origin?) which occasionally and unaccountably beset the island of Madeira had travelled round the coast and the tail-end of it had lashed up against the bathing slabs of Reid's.

In point of fact there was very little actual danger for anyone, but if you were sitting too near the edge you might well be washed out of your deck chair and get a wetting.

Julius Bern, who had always had a horror of drowning, was convinced that his last moment had come and that he would be swept over the edge into the sea. Hooky realized the panic the curious old boy was in and went to his help with a steadying hand and a calming voice.

'There the old so-and-so was screaming blue murder,' Hooky's account of the incident ran, 'and all I did was to pull him on to his feet out of six inches of water and a collapsed deck chair.'

Julius Bern's account of what had happened was different, he was entirely convinced that this powerful, well-built young man springing up from nowhere had saved his life, and although gratitude for favours received was not one of the millionaire's most marked traits he had ever afterwards felt grateful towards Hooky...

'Visiting the flesh-pots,' Hooky answered, 'and you Mr Bern?'

'Making a fool of myself; no sane man ought to drink champagne at three o'clock in the afternoon; but then, perhaps, no sane man ought to get married. Been to Reid's lately? Been saving any more lives?'

Hooky laughed. 'You make too much of that, sir,' he said.

'Do I indeed? I happen not to think so. I suppose you know everybody here?'

'Not everybody. A certain number.'

'Some nice young fillies about; but of course they don't want to waste time with an old crock like me, and they're all snapped up already, anyway. Pity. The older you get the younger you like 'em, and the harder they are to get.'

Hooky smiled in sympathy and drifted away among the constantly moving crowd. His claim to know a certain number of the guests was, of course, justified, the Chanderley wedding was an occasion and it had attracted a colourful sprinkling of the smart young set together with formidable cohorts of the Old Guard. Among the latter Hooky spotted two that he recognised. *Grandames.* Friends of his Aunt; their hats surrealistic, their make-up and jewellery ludicrously lavish. Hooky foresaw boredom on a large scale; but fate saved him; just as the helmeted High Priestesses of the Old Order were closing in on him a voice spoke at his side.

'Enjoying yourself?'

Hooky turned in gratitude; he had lost sight of her for some little time past and now here she was in the nick of time as far as he was concerned and, if he judged her tone of voice right, a shade more friendly than before. Hooky said yes, he was enjoying himself, why not when there was plenty to drink and somebody else was paying for it? 'And you?' he asked.

Virginia laughed and held up a half full glass of champagne.

'Still want to pull everything down?' Hooky asked.

'Of course. Not necessarily at this moment though. Who's that man you were talking to a few moments ago, the one who looks like a piece of warmed up death?'

'That was Mr Julius Bern?'

'A friend of yours?'

'An acquaintance. We move in rather different circles. Julius Bern isn't hard up for the odd ten thousand or so, I am usually hard up for the odd quid.'

'Which of us isn't? I'd like to meet Julius Bern.'

Hooky looked at her in astonishment. 'What on earth do you want to meet Bern for?'

'I saw him the other day in Christie's. Buying a lovely picture. I think, perhaps, he collects pictures.'

'Of course he does. Bern's got one of the best collections of Dutch paintings in London.'

'That's why I want to meet him. I am interested in pictures. Will you introduce me?'

'Of course. How am I to describe you—a distinguished actress or a struggling artist?'

'Don't bother trying to be funny. I'm sure you can be the life and soul of the party; only I don't like your sort of party much. I just want to meet Julius Bern.'

'O.K. There is just one condition, though—'

'What's that?'

'I'm still lonely. Remember I described my plight to you a few glasses back and you weren't particularly sympathetic? I'll introduce you to Bern on condition that you have dinner with me in the near future and tell me how you get on with the old devil; you may be interested in pictures, I'm interested in people; I'd like to hear what you make of him.'

Virginia laughed. 'Fair enough,' she said. 'Yes, I'll have dinner with you one evening. Why not? I've got to eat anyway, so I may as well do it at your expense.'

'A very romantic outlook, I must say.'

'You can leave the romance out of it, just provide the dinner. Give me a ring sometime. 732 04324.'

Hooky produced his Smythson diary and turned to the spare pages at the back of it.

'I'll put you down in List Number Two,' he said, 'the PBP lot.'

'What on earth's that?'

'The Prickly but Possibles; but you never know, after a bit you might graduate into the Welcoming and Willing.'

'My God, the conceit of you men!'

'Frightful isn't it?' Hooky agreed shaking his head. 'Come on we'll go in search of the miserly old millionaire bird and I'll let you loose on him. It will serve him right.'

SEVEN

'A perfectly marvellous idea'

'A ROOM at the top of the block' Len Carron had said. *'A flatlet they call it.'* Virginia had settled into it swiftly and cosily. She was not a great person for possessions, it was part of her philosophy to say she despised them; now, moving about her small room with the miniature cooker in one corner and the bed that let down from the wall and could be folded up out of the way during the day, she thought with amused contempt of the multiplication of things in the Eaton Square drawing-room, the signed photographs, the bits of silver, the enamel snuff boxes, 'God Almighty, what a clutter,' she thought...

Her flatlet was on the third floor; she had not yet troubled to find out anything about the people on the second floor; she was not interested in them, nor in the people on the first floor; her interest was entirely reserved for two rooms on the ground floor where Len Carron lived.

She was thinking about him now as she made casual preparations to get herself a cup of tea. She had had a tiring day and a disappointing one. Not that, in her heart of hearts, she had really expected anything; but the steps up to the agents' offices had been steep; her reception only just on the polite side of indifference; and the eternally off-putting phrases *(absolutely nothing I'm afraid... dead at the moment... if anything should turn up of course—but don't call us, we'll let you know)* had had no comfort in them.

'I thought you were good,' the man she had met at the wedding reception had said. She wasn't certain whether he had really meant it or whether he was just being polite. Not that he looked the sort of man who would bother to be polite just for the sake of it. And in any case she wasn't concerned much with what he thought. *Codswallop* Len had called the play, and she smiled as she remembered; he was right, of course, and she *did* care what Len thought. She cared very much. She cared what he thought about her.

I'm a loner, Len had told her; and she accepted it, had to accept it for the time being. *Men are unwise and curiously planned;* she had read Flecker's *Hassan* at school and, a romantic idealist in those days, had been caught up in the magic of the words. Romanticism had gone, idealism had been twisted, and of the whole once potent play that one line alone had stuck in her mind. *Men are unwise and curiously planned;* then, to get where they want to she thought, women must be wise and must plan even more curiously...

It was a relief to be rid of Roddy Marten; looking back on the episode she found it difficult to decide why she had ever taken up with him. There had been moments of physical excitement between them, but not much else; and even if the bed bits had been satisfactory they didn't make up for the boredom in between. And, of course, that was the truth about Roddy which she could see very clearly now, he was a bore; no edge to him. Len wasn't a bore. There was no possible way in which you could describe Len Carron as a bore. There was frisson with Len. Sparks, a tingling went up and down your spine when you were with him; when you even thought of him. With Roddy she had felt herself in the driving seat and had secretly been contemptuous of him because of it; with Len she didn't want to be in the driving seat, she wanted to be driven.

The kettle started to boil and she moved across towards the tiny stove; on her way back, teapot in hand, she paused for a moment to look out of the window down into the street scene below. She liked this view better than the one at Stanmere Gardens; the 'Gardens' had been scruffy and uninteresting, here there was always some movement of traffic and people.

Not that she liked what she saw at the moment. She disliked it intensely. Her heart sank when she saw the little red car, looking, from her bird's eye view of it, like a toy, a bug, a beetle, a thing that ought to be squashed.

She would have enjoyed squashing it and the woman who drove it. *God, she's here again,* she thought, standing motionless by the window, steaming teapot in hand, tea now forgotten.

Virginia knew her well by sight now: short, fuzzy, mussed up gamine-like hair (the apparently careless result, as any woman would recognise, of careful attention and constant attendance at the hairdresser's); pretty, yes, you had to allow the little bitch that; but pretty in a doll-like way—perhaps Len preferred them doll-like. She didn't believe that, she believed Len liked somebody with brains; presumably he wanted the doll just for bed-play; *I'm a loner;* some loner, Virginia thought, with this fuzzy-haired bit of randiness in and out all the time.

I wonder what they are talking about; now; at this moment! she tormented herself. Me possibly, she thought, they are very probably discussing me... I've met this actress, well, bit of an actress, she's all right; nothing much; nothing like you—Len couldn't be saying that surely, not when he had chosen her to drive the Cortina in the job that Roddy made such a balls of; not when he had said there's a room at the top of this block, it might come in handy at times—futile to imagine what they might be saying to one another. Probably they weren't saying anything, just making animal noises of satisfaction, oh God! . . . in the nursery days at Eaton Square the German governess had always assured them that eavesdroppers never heard any good of themselves; it had been one of a whole range of pious and improving maxims rammed down their throats. . .*sit up, keep your back straight, ladies don't stoop, ladies don't do this, ladies don't do that,* what the hell did ladies do, Virginia had sometimes wondered; *Nanny, what does this mean in the paper—rape?* That's not very nice dear. Ladies don't talk about that sort of thing. . .

I'll bet fuzz doll is finding it nice at this very moment, Virginia thought, and she had hardly formed the thought when to her intense relief fuzz doll stepped out on to the pavement and got into the little red car.

. . . did she move like a woman satisfied? To hell with it if she was satisfied; he hadn't picked her to drive the Cortina; and she hadn't got a marvellous idea to suggest to him. . . I bet she's a bad driver; I hope she runs that damned little red car straight into a bus. . .

Even equipped with a marvellous idea Virginia couldn't bring herself to go down to the ground floor flat at once—there might still be a suggestion of her there, a lingering scent maybe, or something in Len's eyes or in his easy languidness...

When eventually she did go down he was looking at the box.

'Switch that bloody thing off,' he said as she came into the room, 'it's an insult to a man's intelligence.'

Virginia obediently switched off the television asking, as she did so, 'You prefer intelligent things, Len, do you, intelligent people?'

'What do you suppose? I can't be doing with morons, like that man you were shacked up with. God, he turned out a flop all right. Do you know, I believe I could write better stuff myself than half this crap they put on the box. I had a yen for writing once. Still have in a bit of a way. That's why I like the theatre. And that pays dividends sometimes. I wouldn't have gone back stage and met you if I hadn't gone to see that ghastly play you were in.'

'Did you go alone, Len?'

'Mind your own business, Chicky, mind your own business. I've told you, I'm a loner. When I want to be where I want to be alone; when I don't want to be I don't; it's nobody's business but mine—right?'

At least there wasn't any suggestion of scent in the air and she couldn't see even the slightest sign of recent feminine occupation. Len was watching her in amusement. Maybe he guesses what I'm thinking about, she thought; but when finally he spoke it was to ask in a teasing way, 'Been tearing down anything lately, breaking up anything?'

'Not lately, no.'

'I don't get it. You had all the luck; the way you were born you had it all. All you had to do was enjoy it. If I'd been born in Eaton Square I wouldn't be a villain, believe me.'

'I expect you would have been. You'd have gone into the City and been a bigger villain than ever.'

Len laughed at that. 'Could be,' he admitted. 'Let's have a drink.'

'I suppose you need one.'

He shot a sharp look at her. 'What's that supposed to mean?'

'Nothing—only you don't often want a drink.'

'Well I want one now; so get it, will you?'

Virginia moved to a side table and fixed the two drinks; when she came back and handed Len his he said, 'I like watching you, Ginny, I like the way you walk.'

'I never thought you would say a beastly thing like that.'

'Good God, girl, what's the matter now?'

'I can't help it if I limp a little, I can't do anything about my damned foot can I?'

'I wasn't talking about that. I was talking about the rest of you. Tell me about your foot.'

'There's nothing to tell, really. I was born with it. Do you ever read poetry?'

'Poetry? Not as much as I should like to. I wish I'd read more. More of everything. What's poetry got to do with it?'

'What, did the hand then of the Potter shake?—a line out of the Rubá'iyát; with me it obviously did shake.'

'Well, the Potter made a damned good job of the rest of you, anyway.'

Virginia flushed with pleasure at the unexpected compliment. She sat down, took a sip of her drink and looked across at Len over the top of her glass.

He was watching her in amused curiosity.

'What's biting you?' he asked. 'You look as though you're cooking up something.'

'I am Len. I've got what might turn out to be a perfectly marvellous idea.'

'I like girls with ideas; keep talking.'

'Have you ever heard of Julius Bern?'

'Julius Bern?' Carron turned the name over reflectively. 'I've seen his name in the papers. One of these multi-millionaire types isn't he?'

'Very much so. Very millionaire, very multi. Len, this old man has got lots of lovely cash and I thought you would like to get hold of some of it. And I think we might be able to do it.'

'We?'

'You can't do it without me, Len.'

Carron took a swig from his drink and set the glass down carefully on the broad arm of his chair. 'Don't try holding a pistol at my head, chick,' he said. 'People who do that are apt to come unstuck. What's this wonderful scheme of yours, then? Do you know this Julius Bern?'

'Yes I do. I've been introduced to him. I saw him at Christie's, the auction place, some weeks ago. I didn't know him then, I just happened to see him. He paid two hundred and fifty thousand pounds for a picture.'

'A quarter of a million for a picture—he must be crackers.'

'He *is* crackers over his pictures, that's the essence of the thing. When I went to my sister's wedding reception there were lots of people I knew, of course, and lots more I didn't. One of the men I didn't know came up and talked about that play I was in; said he thought I was good in it and generally chatted me up a bit. I had no objection to that naturally, although I didn't go all that much on this particular character; he seemed a bit too sure of himself, there was a bit too much of the men-are-lords-of-creation air about him.'

'You're not going to start any women's lib stuff with me, are you.'

'What I'm trying to start, Len, is a super idea for getting hold of some cash, and an idea with a bit of excitement in it too, if only you'll let me explain—'

'O.K. Carry on.'

'When this look-at-the-lovely-hairs-on-my-chest type started on the bit about being lonely and wouldn't I have dinner with him some evening I slid away, I wasn't particularly interested.'

'So he'll have to show his manly chest to somebody else eh?'

'No, he won't. Ten minutes after we had been chatting together I caught sight of him again. Across the other side of the room. Talking to Julius Bern. So I made my way through the mob to him and picked up the conversation where we had left off. It turns out that he is a friend of Bern's and in return for a dinner date he introduced me to him.'

'What did you want to be introduced to Bern for?'

'This picture that he bought at Christie's, *Woman with a Flageolet*—'

'Woman with a what?'

'Flageolet.'

'What the heck's that?'

'Something to do with music. I thought it must be something kinky at first,' Virginia laughed, 'but it turns out to be a kind of musical instrument; anyway, Julius Bern is mad on pictures it appears and this *Woman with a Flageolet* is going to be one of his greatest treasures.'

'It damned well ought to be at a quarter of a million quid.'

'And if he lost it he would very likely give quite a lot to get it back again, don't you think?'

'If he lost it?' There was a slight change in the inflection of Carron's voice which told the girl that he was beginning to be interested. 'How's he going to do that?'

'I haven't any idea yet; but this hairy-chest type—Hefferman his name is—introduced me to Bern and I spun a yarn about being an art student and interested in pictures; actually it's half true, I did study art for a bit. Once inside Bern's house I can get to work. He looks to me as though he might be a dirty old man; most men tend to be after a certain age. Of course it may all come to nothing, but if I make myself as nice as I know how to him and tell him I'm willing to go up and look at his pictures any time he wants I might be able to work out something, don't you think?'

Len nodded. 'You might indeed,' he agreed. 'It's worth a try.'

'At any rate I could find out where all the pictures are and what safety precautions are taken to look after them and what the household staff consists of and so on, couldn't I?'

'You certainly could. You may have an idea there, Ginny. You had better keep on the right side of this guy and start things moving. Good girl. Ten out of ten for a bright idea.'

'I thought you would be interested, Len.'

'Don't lose your virtue more often than necessary.'

'Perhaps I could say the same to you.'

'You could say it, chick, but it wouldn't make any difference. Don't worry about me, just get on with the job and we'll see if we can't work out something together.'

EIGHT

Sitting up at the bar

VIRGINIA HAD not so much as seen Len Carron for three days; he hadn't said anything about going away, not given a hint that he wouldn't be there; he just *wasn't* there; the two rooms on the ground floor were suddenly unoccupied; no response to the bell and the milk bottles accumulating outside the door.

... he might at least have told me he was off somewhere Virginia tormented herself, *he might have said a word—but why should he? Of course he wouldn't; he isn't like that; Len doesn't really give a damn about me—yet; but he will; to hell with Len Carron and that red-headed bitch he has probably gone off with, somewhere in the Home Counties I expect, the Compleat Angler at Marlow probably; somewhere like that; oh God...*

The ringing of the telephone came as a relief; something else to think about; unless, of course—she hurried her steps across the room—unless it was by any chance Len—

It wasn't Len; not by any chance...

'Hooky Hefferman here. Remember me? The kindly, accommodating type who was so nice to you at your sister's wedding do. Good-looking too, in a rough sort of way, or so they tell me.'

Virginia cut in with, 'I wouldn't believe them if I were you,' but she couldn't help smiling slightly.

'May be you're right there,' Hooky agreed. 'I was wondering how you got on with your millionaire art friend.'

'I haven't been up to see his pictures yet. I'm going next Friday.'

'Ah, pity. I was hoping to have a long account of it over dinner this evening.'

'Are you asking me out to dinner?'

'Nowhere grand, mind you; you might start pulling the place down.'

'God, your humour does creak doesn't it? You want to get someone to do a re-write job on your dialogue.'

'I forgot I was talking to a stage expert.'

'Sarcastic bastard.'

'Well, after this exchange of compliments, what about dinner?'

'Of course I'll come. I'm bored to tears.'

'Where do I call for you?'

'You don't. We'll meet. Nowhere grand, like you said. I want a place where we can sit up at the bar on high stools and eat something cold and tasty. You must know lots of pubs—'

'Too many; if I were to give you a list—'

'Don't, for heavens sake. I'm not interested. Just mention one for this evening.'

'The Good Soldier in Grafton Street. What is it now? Half past seven? I'll be there waiting at eight o'clock. O.K.?'

'You'll probably still be waiting at twenty past eight. I'm not a very punctual person. I have my own ideas about time.'

'Does Time know?'

'Oh God, those wise-cracks again! I'll be there. Bag two stools at the bar.'

The clock said eight fifteen when the door of the saloon bar opened and she stood for a moment hesitant on the threshold. To anyone who could read them right those three seconds of hesitation were an interesting clue to Virginia's character. In spite of her youthful willingness to storm the Bastilles of the modern world the truth, the cold truth, was that the girl was still in some ways a little shy. On entering a room alone she always had this moment of hesitation. She knew she ought not to have it. She was an actress. She ought to be able to make an entrance. She knew all the things she ought to do and ought to be glad to do, but the suspicion of shyness, the disturbing little shadow of self-doubt which she had never confessed to anyone, was still persistently there.

She caught sight of the square shouldered figure sitting up at the bar and was at once reassured. Someone she knew. A professional chatter-up of attractive girls maybe, but still someone she knew; and someone amusing to talk to; someone she could enjoy quarrelling with; much better fun keeping this masculine extrovert at arm's length than sitting alone in the flat waiting for the hated little red car to pull up in the street below...

'Congratulations,' Hooky said. 'You're five minutes ahead of your schedule.'

'What on earth does five minutes matter one way or the other?'

'How right you are. It doesn't matter. Time is an illusion. As my old chum Chu Ling has it *"the bird of Eternal Truth struggles unsuccessfully in the confusing net of Time".*'

'Chu Ling?'

'He ran a Take Away Philosophical Stall in the market place of Pekin about a thousand years ago or maybe it was two thousand. What's a few hundred years between friends? I like that outfit you're wearing. Green suits you, you look nice in it.'

'I imagine that is one of your standard lines of approach, isn't it?'

Hooky nodded vigorously. 'Absolutely. Show a girl that you are aware of what she's wearing and you've scored a point. She may even take it off for you. Women like men to notice their clothes.'

Virginia laughed, partly at herself; it was perfectly true that any woman liked to be told that she was looking nice; and incidentally it was also perfectly true that green suited her. Green was her colour.

'I see you managed to get two stools at the bar,' she said.

'As per instructions. I'm a great one for carrying out instructions. Place your shapely little behind on the stool I've been keeping for you and tell me if you approve of lobster and a bottle of Rüdesheimer Hock.'

'That sounds fine to me.'

'I'll endeavour to attract Cyril's attention. Cyril is a first-rate barman when he is not thinking of other things. Unfortunately he very frequently *is* thinking of other things. His mind browses delicately among sensuous images.'

Virginia eyed the barman, busy at the other end of the bar, with interest. 'Len hates them,' she said at length.

'Len?'

'Somebody who hates poufs.'

'A friend of yours?'

'Mind your own business.'

Hooky smiled amiably. It crossed his mind that to administer a few resounding slaps to the taut little bottom which had just perched itself on the stool next to his might in time become necessary and would indeed be an agreeable task. But at the moment he was under instructions and as he himself had just pointed out he was a great man for carrying out instructions.

Cyril, detaching his mind from goodness knows what engaging sensuous images, produced lobster and a bottle of ice-cold Rüdesheimer.

'So you haven't paid a visit to our friend J.B. yet?' Hooky asked.

'Not yet. I'm going next Friday. When you introduced me to him at that wedding affair of my sister's we had quite a long talk together. We got on famously. Incidentally how did you come to know him?'

'We were fellow guests at a place you wouldn't approve of at all. Reid's Hotel in Madeira. The old boy had trouble with his deck-chair and I heroically went to his rescue.'

'Some hero, rescuing people out of collapsed deck-chairs.'

'As you rightly say, some hero. And you are really interested in Bern's pictures?'

'Of course I am. I was an artist myself once.'

'A girl of many talents. So what do you want to pull everything down for?'

'An artist would have made the world differently.'

'You better have a word with God.'

'Is the lobster all right?' Cyril enquired. 'Is it to Madam's liking?'

'It's delicious,' Virginia assured him, smiling. Len could say what he liked about them but she found Cyril's sort attractive; as most women did...Len was intolerant, of course, but then that was what made him Len; nothing wishy-washy, half and half about him; take it or leave it with Len; come my way or get out...*I hope he's telling that red-headed bitch to get out of it at this very moment, I hope he's good and intolerant with her...*

'Are you a tolerant sort of person?' she asked Hooky, 'or wildly, madly intolerant? Tell me about yourself. I'm interested. I know why you are interested in me. For the obvious reason. That's what's so boring about men. They're so god-damned obvious. Well, you're not going to get me into bed for a very long time; if ever. What do you do for a living? Don't tell me. I'll guess. You're something in the P.R. racket, that's just about your mark, I'd say.'

'I'm in the literary world,' Hooky informed her. 'Well, the illiterate world really, Fleet Street. I'm the racing correspondent of the *Church Times.*'

Virginia sighed. 'You don't write the corny gags for these so-called comedies on the box do you?' she asked.

'I'm working down towards that,' Hooky said, 'but seriously I am a bit of a writer and I am genuinely interested in the theatre. That's why I came up and spokc to you at your sister's wedding. One of the coloured supplements wants a series of articles on the sixty per cent of the acting profession which is said to be always out of work; what a talented young actress like yourself does when she's out of a job; where she lives and how she lives; her friends and amusements—all that sort of thing.'

Virginia studied him for a moment and said, 'I never know whether to take you seriously or not.'

'Uncertainty is the spice of life,' Hooky pointed out. 'As the bishop said to the actress it's amusing to speculate what's going to happen next. Cyril dig out another bottle of this excellent hock, will you?'

Virginia had no objection at all to a second bottle of Rüdesheimer being opened. She liked wine and she was finding the evening amusing. Len? For the moment to hell with Len; presumably Len was enjoying himself with his doll-like, over-dressed bit... why was it that all men—especially a man like Len—fell for the woman who overdid everything? Plastered it on: make-up, mascara, scent... but however she tarted herself up the red-headed bit didn't have a marvellous scheme to put up to Len about the things that really interested him; she might wave her open arms and legs at him for the time being but he'd get tired of her; he'd come round; so to hell with Len for the moment, for this evening anyway. She was finding the racing correspondent of the *Church Times* amusing; maybe his talk of a series for one of the coloured supplements was genuine; difficult to tell with this guy whether he was fooling or not . . .

'And where are you living at the moment, then?' Hooky asked conversationally.

'Not in Eaton Square.'

'Very wise too. The young ought to leave the nest as soon as they can and set up on their own.'

'That's exactly what I've done.'

'All on your own?'

'Don't be so damned inquisitive.'

Hooky laughed in genuine amusement; he could see how right he had been to suggest the Prickly-but-Possible list for this spirited filly; but that was the way he liked them; no spirit, no fun.

'I must be inquisitive,' he pointed out. 'How can I write about you if I don't see you in your usual surroundings, birds must be studied in their natural habitat, that's rule one of your ardent ornithologists.'

'Ardent, not to say randy, I can believe; ornithologist I'll take a hell of a lot of persuading about.'

'Len, I take it, is not an ornithologist?'

Virginia held out her glass for the attentive Cyril to replenish it. Watching the flow of bland wine she smiled. She was tempted to say *Len is a villain; he's on the outside; he hasn't swallowed the dope; he knows it's all a racket; it's a scrum and he's in there fighting hard for what he can get out of it.* To her own surprise what she found herself saying was 'Len's a bit like you in a way, I'd say.'

'No wonder you find him attractive.'

'Good grief, the conceit of the man! And who said I find Len attractive anyway?'

'I was just guessing.'

'Keep on guessing, sailor; it's as near as you'll get.' She held up her glass and considered the effect of light filtering through the amber liquid. 'And if you really want to know, if you really are doing that article you talked about, yes, I *do* find him attractive. As attractive as hell. I'm fond of him. Fond? What a stupid word. Words are hopelessly inadequate things, anyway. *Fond!* when you're tortured thinking what he might be saying, doing, at this very moment. To hell with him anyway. Fond. It's like "*sorry*"—when Alec was killed people came up to me and said they were *sorry*—'

'Alec?' Hooky asked gently.

'In Northern Ireland. My brother. They sent him to Sandhurst so of course he was a soldier. I suppose he was a good one. What's the name of this pub we are in—The Good Soldier? God, there isn't such a thing. Alec and I weren't twins but we couldn't have been closer if we had been. He went over with his regiment to Northern Ireland to try and persuade the stupid Protestants not to kill the lunatic Catholics and the lunatic Catholics not to kill the stupid Protestants which they were busy doing. All in the name of religion, of course. God must be laughing his head off up there. Or crying his eyes out. Anyway this house was blazing away, set on fire on sound religious principles naturally, and apparently Alec thought there was a woman inside so he went in to see what he could do; but instead of a woman there was a booby trap and he got blown to pieces. They couldn't even bury him, not properly.'

'I'm sorry.'

The girl gave a hard, dry laugh. 'There you are. You're at it now. You're sorry. O.K. O.K. I know what you mean. It's just that words are inadequate. I was sorry too. You can put that in your article. When her brother was killed, blown into little pieces, in a war which means nothing and can't settle anything anyway, she was sorry. You can put that in.'

'O.K. I will. And I'll also put in Alec's parents were sorry, too; and would have liked the girl to stay at home to help comfort them.'

Virginia became alerted. 'You're not on a salvation job, are you?' she asked. 'You're not trying to get me back to Eaton Square?'

'Do I look like a salvationist?'

'You look like a typical chauvinist hoping to get a girl into bed with him.'

'You couldn't possibly have summed it up better.'

'Go on hoping.'

'Meanwhile may I have the pleasure of running you home?'

'As far as the front door.'

'I've known front doors to open before now.'

They slid off their high stools.

'I hope everything was to Madam's satisfaction,' Cyril said.

'I enjoyed it all enormously,' Virginia answered. 'Even some of the conversation.'

'And sir, too?' Cyril enquired.

'I'm a great student of human nature,' Hooky told him, 'and I find myself learning all the time.'

When he brought his car to a halt outside Virginia's block of flats Hooky, wise old campaigner, had the sense not to push his luck. Softlee, softlee. He didn't even suggest that he might be asked inside; he had, after all, discovered where the girl lived, he had tracked her to her lair and for the moment that would have to suffice; but grappling hooks could be prepared for the future. As Virginia was getting out of the car he said, 'I shall be most interested to hear what you think of Bern's pictures.'

'Why? You aren't an artist.'

PBP. indeed, Hooky thought, hedgehogs aren't in it with this little bundle of awkwardness. He smiled sweetly at her. 'No, I'm not; but it is your opinion of the pictures I'm anxious to hear; I should like to hear you discuss them. What about another visit to *The Good Soldier* sometime soon?'

'I hate tying myself up in advance, fixing dates, making arrangements, writing things down in an engagement book, all that sort of thing; that's all so incredibly bourgeois and boring.'

'Well, without being so bourgeois as to write anything down, if I were to give you a ring some day and say what about another visit to Cyril for lobster and hock you might conceivably say yes. Right?'

The hated little red car was standing in the forecourt of the flats and Virginia, with a sinking heart, had suddenly caught sight of it. She turned to Hooky and in a changed tone of voice said abruptly, 'Yes. I'll come out with you again. Give me a ring in a day or two.'

Hooky watched her walk away from the car and disappear through the front door of the flats with some bewilderment; what had made her change her mind so quickly, he wondered, and why that change of voice, what the devil had bitten her all of a sudden?...

NINE

St John's Wood

LESSING CAME into the kitchen carrying a tray with the post-luncheon coffee things on it.

'He says there's a young lady coming to tea so to be certain there's something nice in the way of cakes and so on.'

Mrs Lessing made a slight grimace. 'Him and his young ladies!' she said. 'You'd really think he would know better at his age wouldn't you?'

Lessing laughed. 'It's his age that's the trouble,' he said. 'Shall we be all right for cakes?'

'Yes, of course we will. If somebody's coming to tea I'll see there's a proper tea. You can leave all that to me. What happens after tea is none of my business, thank goodness.'

'Then I wouldn't worry about it if I was you,' her husband advised sharply. He sat down, poured out a cup of coffee for himself and lit a cigarette.

Julius Bern was a fanatical non-smoker. He hated the smell of tobacco and any suggestion of smoking was strictly taboo on the house side of the green baize door; nobody was better aware of this than Bern's manservant Albert Lessing, but in Pine Place the green baize door was a frontier which in one direction was never crossed.

When he had bought the house, ten years ago, Bern had once gone all over it very thoroughly. As he himself said he didn't believe in buying a pig in a poke. It was a very expensive pig and before moving in he made it into a very comfortable poke.

Once he was established in the house, and once Albert Lessing and his wife were installed there to look after him, Bern never again went near the domestic quarters. Nor, although he was in many respects a miser, did he ask to see any household bills or accounts. Like many rich men Bern hated spending money on things he regarded as unnecessary or undesirable. Occasionally a business rival, or somebody seeking a favour of some kind, would mistakenly invite him to lunch at one of the most expensive restaurants in the West End; the resultant bill, perhaps thirty pounds for the two of them, always horrified Bern who, if by himself, would happily have gone to a café and had scrambled eggs on toast and a cup of coffee. Incidentally the expensive luncheon was apt to be self-defeating—if a man was fool enough to spend that amount of money on a single meal he was not likely to be a suitable person to do business with.

But when he wanted a thing (*Woman with a Flageolet* for example) Bern was ready to spend money on it. What he wanted in Pine Place was complete freedom from domesticity. He didn't want to know what wages individual servants were paid; he didn't want to hear about bills from the butcher, the baker and the candlestick maker; so long as his own modest and sometimes curious wants were looked after and so long as he was never bothered about anything he had no further interest in what happened on the kitchen side of the green baize door.

Julius Bern's method of securing this happy state of things was simple, and its effective simplicity was typical of the man.

All the troublesome work was done at the outset—a searchingly rigorous vetting and interviewing of possible candidates. Once the choice was made the rest was easy.

Albert Lessing and his wife were engaged and the conditions were made plain to them: they were to look after the house and Bern himself in the capacity of manservant and cook; they were to employ and pay what daily help they found necessary; they were to order and pay for all food; they were to provide Bern with what he wanted (it turned out to be very little) when he wanted it (he turned out to have remarkably fixed habits); they were not to bring domestic problems or worries out of the kitchen quarters.

In order that the Lessings could do this effectively and that he could have a completely troublefree background to the curious sort of life he led Bern paid his manservant yearly the sum of nine thousand pounds. It represented rather less than one fortieth part of his annual income; 'two and a half per cent for comfort and absence of worry,' he would sometimes say with a self-congratulatory chuckle, 'well worth it, cheap at the price.'

Albert Lessing was not the sort of person either to underestimate his good fortune or to abuse it. He was a very good manservant indeed, far too good to show curiosity about any peculiar habits his employer might have; in Albert Lessing's opinion a man who had the sort of income Julius Bern enjoyed and who had enough sense to have his household managed on such practical lines was entitled to his little peculiarities.

'You'll have to let Goddard know there's somebody coming,' Mrs Lessing reminded her husband.

Lessing nodded and presently went out into the grounds in search of the day-time security man.

Pine Place, an Edwardian house, had not got extensive grounds by any standard but, thickly planted with trees and shrubs, they were sufficient to give it privacy from the quiet residential road in which it stood.

Bern's policy towards the domestic side of his house was mirrored by his attitude towards privacy. He employed two security men at wages a good deal higher than they would get anywhere else. Goddard was on duty in the day time, Williams at night. Their orders were not to let anyone approach the house who was not 'on the list' i.e. a known regular such as the postman, the milkman, and the like, or someone whose advent they had been told to expect. Anyone outside these categories was intercepted and questioned; they might, or might not, be allowed to proceed; in any case warning would be given by telephone to the house and the security man on duty would accompany the visitor to the front door. In addition the gallery in which Bern's treasured Dutch pictures were hung was fitted with a 'direct police alarm'—the only entrance was by the door, when the door was opened an alarm bell rang instantly in the police station in Acacia Road.

Goddard was a burly, active man not yet forty who, like the butler, knew that he had a good billet and intended to keep it. Zena, the Alsatian bitch, was at his side when Lessing came out to speak to him.

'There's a visitor coming to tea, Fred. A young lady. Miss Cave. Round about four. She's O.K.'

Goddard nodded. 'A young lady, eh? Up to his little games again is he?'

Both men laughed, but Lessing didn't feel inclined to take up the conversation, he didn't believe in criticism of his employer.

'She's coming to look at Mr Bern's pictures,' he said.

'And I can't say that surprises me,' Goddard answered with a wink.

Virginia took the Bakerloo line to St John's Wood Station and from there made her way to Acacia Road. She had made herself up and dressed carefully for the occasion, on the assumption that Julius Bern would probably be after what in her experience most men, to a greater or lesser degree, were after.

Acacia Road wasn't difficult to find and Virginia approved of the quietness of it and the absence of traffic; as yet she had not even the beginnings of a plan but she had the general feeling that the quieter and more obviously residential the road was the better.

At Pine Place she got a shock. The house stood back a little, separated from the road by a small front garden and, indeed, largely hidden by well-grown trees and shrubs. She had scarcely opened the ornamental iron gate which led from footpath to garden before she was confronted by a powerful looking figure coming suddenly into view from behind the cover of a bush.

A tough looking man holding an Alsatian dog on a lead.

As it happened Virginia disliked all dogs, and had a strong antipathy to Alsatians.

'Oh!' she exclaimed.

Goddard smiled, he enjoyed making people jump. 'Sorry if I startled you, Miss. Miss Cave is it? That's O.K. then, you're expected. Stop growling Zena. Don't worry about Zena, Miss, she just doesn't like strangers. Ring the front door bell and you'll be O.K.' He watched Virginia walk up the short path to the house and thought his own private amused thoughts...*a real bit of stuff this one, that randy old man will overdo it one day, especially at his age*...

Virginia, having recovered from the momentary scare of the Alsatian, was enjoying herself. Like all people of the theatre she was, in effect, always on the stage, she always thought of herself as being in a part. And this part was exciting. Len approved of this part...*keep your eyes open,* Len had said, *let's learn all we can about the place, all the details*... so far, then, one bodyguard type in the gardens with that blasted dog... The door was opened to her by another man. Quite unmistakably the butler. Spiritual brother to his counterpart in Eaton Square. What other staff was there, Virginia wondered...

'Miss Cave? Mr Bern is expecting you, Miss.'

Virginia followed Lessing across a fair-sized hall into the drawing room and was announced by him.

The day was by no means cold but there was a coal fire burning in the grate; Julius Bern liked warmth and didn't believe in economising in it.

He was affability itself, overdoing it in fact, as lecherous old men are inclined to with attractive young women. Virginia recognised the affability for exactly what it was, and she welcomed it, the mood from which it sprang was going to make things so much easier for her. Her enjoyment increased, it was all going to be fun and exciting; it was all going to be something that would please Len...

The room was overcrowded with heavy French furniture. Stuff which Virginia disliked intensely; it reminded her of a childhood visit to the Rothschilds' house at Waddesdon...*possessions* she thought...nothing of any use to Len here...she glanced round the walls; a medium sized mirror hung on one side of the fireplace and there were three pictures, but no *Woman with a Flageolet,* she noticed... Tea was brought in on a large silver tray. Small, delicately cut triangular sandwiches and chocolate biscuits and a luscious cake.

'What a marvellous tea!' Virginia exclaimed as the door closed behind Lessing.

'They look after me pretty well,' Bern said complacently, 'and I warned them somebody special was coming.'

'I suppose you have a large staff in a house like this?'

Bern laughed, amused in a masculine way at the naïveté of the young. 'Oh Lord no. You don't need a large staff to be comfortable. That's just an illusion. One of the many illusions most people live their lives by. I don't live by illusions. All I need to be comfortable is a really good man and wife and as many daily women as they like to engage. Two, I think it is. I don't know or care. I suppose they do the scrubbing and dusting and so on. A lot of servants mean a lot of trouble. And I don't like trouble. Too old to like trouble.'

Virginia duly laughed incredulously as she knew she was expected to at the mere mention of age. She wanted to go on to ask about the outdoor staff, the ex-bruiser type with the Alsatian in the garden, but she thought she had better wait...don't do anything to rouse the old goat's suspicions, Len had counselled, don't ask too many questions all at once...

'...but I didn't ask you up here to bore you with talk about my domestic staff,' Bern was saying. 'I wanted to talk about you, Miss Cave, Virginia isn't it?'

'Yes that's right, Virginia.'

'You don't think an old man rude for using your Christian name?'

Old, old, too old, God how they keep harping on age when they are past it Virginia thought.

Smiling brightly and reassuringly she answered. 'Of course I don't; and in any case I simply can't think of you as old, Mr Bern.'

'Julius. What a nice thing to say. Well, perhaps I'm not entirely an extinct volcano.'

Virginia continued to smile at him encouragingly. *I'll bet you're not,* she thought...

'...and now let's talk about you. You're interested in pictures?'

'Yes. Very much so. I was an art student once. For nearly two years; in Sobert's atelier.'

'Then you are an artist.'

'No. Not really. I gave it up. But I've always been intensely interested in anything to do with pictures. Especially the Dutch school.'

'And how did you come to know that I, too, was interested in the Dutch school?'

'I was at Christie's when you bought the *Woman with a Flageolet.*'

'Were you indeed? And were you there to bid for it as well?'

'Good heavens no! But I often go there when there's a sale of pictures on. I saw you buy it and I thought how marvellous it must be to own such a lovely picture.'

'And you would like to see it again?'

'I should love to.'

'Well, let's finish our tea first shall we, my dear young lady. Mrs Lessing will be disappointed if you don't eat some of her excellent cake.'

During tea Bern asked Virginia some questions about herself, and in reply she lied fluently and cheerfully and thoroughly enjoyed doing it.

It appeared that she shared a flat with two other girls, both of whom had good secretarial posts, and that at the moment there wasn't any man she was particularly interested in (she offered a mental apology to Len as she made this reassuring statement to her host).

'What about the young man who introduced you to me?' Bern asked.

'Him? Oh I hardly know him at all.'

'I should have thought he was the type who would be very attractive to women.'

'Personally I far prefer older men, like you, Mr Bern.'

'Julius.'

'Like you, Julius.'

'So perhaps you'll find time to come and visit me occasionally?'

'Of course I will. I should love to. I expect you get quite lonely sometimes don't you?'

'Very.'

'You ought to have a dog. Do you have a dog? I saw one in the garden with a man.'

'I don't like animals. Messy, demanding things. That would be Goddard in the garden with the dog; one of the security men.'

'*One* of them?' Virginia laughed brightly. 'However many have you got, then?'

'Only two. One by day, one by night. A good man and a dog are quite enough to deal with unwanted people. And of course the house is not without safety precautions as you can imagine.'

I'll bet it isn't, Virginia thought. *I'll bet you've got precautions for your precious possessions but what the hell are they, that's what Len will want to know...*

She declined a second cup of tea and Bern leant across her to take her cup and put it on the tray. It was an unnecessary gesture and he deliberately took an unnecessary time over it, contriving to press with his forearm against the warm softness of her breast in the movement.

Virginia replied by moving her body forward very slightly but unmistakably against the pressure of his arm; when their eyes met for a second she smiled at him. This was the sort of development she had hoped for and she was delighted by it; *silly old fool,* she thought. *God they never think they're past it do they*. . . if Julius Bern turned out to be d.o.m. she reckoned that she wouldn't have much difficulty in pulling the wool over his eyes . . .

Bern put her cup on the silver tray and resumed his seated position slowly.

'And now if you would really like to see my pictures,' he said, 'we'll go up to the gallery.' He pressed a bell-push and Lessing came in.

'I'm taking Miss Cave up to the gallery,' Bern told him. 'Clear the tea things and,' he gave a quick nod, 'so on.'

'Very good, Sir.'

Just as she was going through the doorway Virginia happened to glance back and she noticed something that struck her as odd—the butler's first move in clearing the tea tray away was to take down the mirror that hung on one side of the fireplace and to lay it carefully on a small side table that stood beneath it . . .

'It's not a grand house,' Bern was saying as he led the way up the elegant little staircase, 'I don't like grand things, I like good things. This is the gallery, here.'

He opened a door at the end of the corridor and stood aside to let Virginia in.

'Don't you keep it locked?' Virginia asked.

Bern laughed. 'Don't worry,' he said. 'Except when I want to go in through it this door is very securely locked indeed, and guarded in other ways; quite a lot of things would happen if anyone who wasn't supposed to opened this door.'

He led the way in and Virginia followed.

The gallery, which was long and comparatively narrow, had been made by knocking two existing bedrooms together and building on an extension; there were no windows, the room was lit entirely artificially by four long strips of neon lighting. Not more than a score of pictures hung on the walls, all of the Dutch school, all by master painters. *Woman with Flageolet* occupied a more or less central position on the left hand wall but as he was quick to explain, Bern hadn't yet decided where it would finally go.

'I shall have to rearrange things a bit,' he said, 'but of course that's part, a large part, of the enjoyment—to be constantly handling the paintings, seeing them in a fresh position, literally in a fresh light and in juxtaposition with new neighbours. I'm sure I don't have to tell you, my dear young lady, you being an artist yourself, that you don't "see" a picture just by looking at it once; you have to live with it a long time before you really come to know it.'

Virginia studied the van Dysen without speaking for a couple of minutes. It was a masterpiece and, like all masterpieces which man has managed to achieve—Lear, Beethoven's Ninth, King's College Chapel—it had the effect of imposing silence and inhibiting comment.

At last she did speak. 'It's lovely,' she said; she meant what she said, but at the same time she was also thinking 'it *is* lovely; and he paid a quarter of a million for it, two hundred and fifty thousand pounds! I wonder what he'll pay to get it back. . .'

Bern was perfectly sincere in his devotion to his Dutch pictures, but they were there all the time, he could enjoy them whenever he wanted to, and by himself. The Dutch pictures satisfied his passion for masterly painting; but there were other passions; being a man, a forked-radish procreating creature, he was shaken by, slave to, another passion. The Dutch pictures were not the only ones he enjoyed looking at. He had another collection in a small room beyond the far end of the gallery, an intimate private collection; not for public display; to be enjoyed by himself alone when in a certain mood, in the grip of a certain passion; or better still, if he was lucky enough to be able to contrive it so, to be enjoyed in the company of a young, eager girl. But, of course, he had to go slowly; he realised that; and in a way going slowly was half the fun; he had been clever enough—as he saw it—to persuade this attractive girl to come up and visit him; he flattered himself that he had made a little headway with her—that moment when he had deliberately leant across and against her, pretending to reach for her cup, she had quite definitely responded to that—she would come up again, he was sure of it, so there was no need to rush things now; still it was always useful, and titillating, to put in a little preliminary work—

'Of course these aren't my only pictures.'

'Don't tell me you've got *more?*'

Bern indicated the door at the end of the gallery.

'There's a smaller room through there, oh an altogether smaller room, you wouldn't call it a gallery at all; but it houses a rather special collection; some drawings some photographs.'

'Can I see them?'

Bern considered; it was tempting to say 'yes', but half the fun of the thing was anticipation.

'As I say it's rather a special collection; a specialised subject; I'm not altogether sure that you would enjoy them.'

Virginia smiled at him. 'I'm sure I should,' she said.

She realised that the d.o.m. hypothesis was proving abundantly right; if Julius Bern, aged what? sixty-eight, seventy she guessed, probably now impotent, had a collection of erotica and got his kicks showing it to a girl about a third of his age—why then that suited her book splendidly. Men in that frame of mind were easy game. But she remembered Len's advice, don't rush at it, don't scare him off, take it easy...

So when Bern said, 'Perhaps you will cheer an old man up by coming to tea again soon, and then, if you still feel curious about my little private collection—' Virginia answered, 'of course I'll come again. I'd love to. And I can't wait to see your special pictures. I look forward to that.'

On the way downstairs Virginia did some quick thinking. When they reached the hall she said, 'Mr Bern, Julius, I wonder if I might ask a favour of you, a real favour.'

'Of course. Anything you like, my dear.'

'I'm mad about that van Dysen. Would you let me make a copy of it?'

Bern laughed. 'You can make as many copies of it as you like,' he assured her.

'It's such a marvellous painting; if you would just let me sit in that wonderful gallery of yours and do my best to reproduce it; and when I've finished working on that perhaps you would show me those special things in the little room?'

'When do you want to come?'

'Would next Wednesday suit, in the afternoon?'

'I'll tell Goddard and Lessing to expect you.'

VIRGINIA WAS sitting with Len in the living room of his flat... the red-head had not been around lately; possibly, oh blissful thought, Len had got tired of her, you never knew with Len when a sudden change of mood would seize him; today he was more friendly than usual and anxious to hear about Pine Place.

'How did you get on up there, then?' he asked.

Virginia's eyes shone with suppressed excitement; she felt like saying *marvellously,* but she had learnt that it didn't do to show too much enthusiasm with Len. All the same, inside, she felt enthusiastic; she was enjoying herself just as she had been when she listened to Len planning the abortive wage snatch; now she was doing the planning...

'How did you get on up there then?' Len asked. 'What sort of a joint is it?'

'It's tucked away in one of those quiet, expensive St John's Wood roads.'

'Detached?'

'Oh Lord, yes; in its own grounds. Must have cost the earth to buy.'

'That wouldn't worry Bern. Large grounds?'

'Not very. On the small side, actually. Trees and shrubs and a bit of lawn. Plenty of spaces to hide if we wanted to. The first thing that happens as soon as you get inside the gate, is that a man with a huge Alsatian dog appears and wants to know who you are and so on. I hate dogs, especially Alsatians.'

Len was genuinely surprised. 'Hate dogs? I love them. I should have thought you would too, with your upbringing.'

'Well, I don't and I never have done.'

'O.K. don't get steamed up. So there's a security patrol; well, there naturally would be.'

'There are two actually; one, during the day, one at night. And presumably two dogs, as well.'

'Forget the dogs. Was this security man armed?'

'He could have been. I don't know. He looked a pretty tough type anyway.'

Len nodded; he expected a security man to be tough, probably an ex-pug or ex-policeman; even possibly an ex-convict, poacher turned gamekeeper, often the hardest sort to deal with, they knew the tricks. Anyway he was a man, human, and therefore in some degree or other, in some manner or other, he would be vulnerable; that was a point which might have to be considered later; meanwhile—

'And this security character takes you up to the front door presumably and waits whilst he gets the O.K. about you?'

'Yes. They knew I was coming, of course, so I swanned in.'

'What's the staff inside?'

'The minimum. A butler and his wife—I didn't see her—and two daily women. Apparently Julius—'

Len interrupted her with a laugh. 'Julius eh? You seem to have got on pretty good terms with the old bastard already.'

'Of course I have. That was the whole idea, surely?'

Len nodded, smiling. 'So the house isn't stuffed with servants?' he prompted.

'Virtually only the two of them. Julius has got a thing about it. As long as he's well fed and warm and comfortable he simply doesn't want to know what happens in the kitchen department, "the other side of the baize door" he calls it.'

'Just how I should behave if I had his money,' Len said approvingly. 'Did you see the picture?'

'Yes, of course. After tea. We went up to what he called "the gallery". It looks as though two rooms may have been knocked into one. Long and narrow. No windows. Strip lighting and about twenty pictures in it. All Dutch.'

'And the one we are after—what's it called?'

'Woman with a Flageolet.'

'Was that there?'

'Yes, indeed it was. Not yet in its final position Julius says, he's thinking that out. It's a beautiful picture, Len.'

'Let's hope it will be worth a lot of beautiful money to us,' Len said. 'What about locks and so on, on the door of this gallery place?'

'I was on the lookout for that. He certainly didn't unlock the door. He just turned the handle and we went in; but he did say that unless he wanted to use the door it was very securely locked indeed, and that if anyone who wasn't supposed to, opened it—as he put it—*quite a lot of things would happen.*'

Len nodded; it was what he expected.

'There'll be an alarm system of some kind,' he said, 'sure to be. Probably sets off a hooter in the house and simultaneously rings in the local police station. But, of course, alarm systems have to be capable of being switched off as well as on. Where is this gallery, at the end of a corridor, you said?'

'Yes, at the end of a short corridor.'

'Going along the corridor did you notice Bern do anything that might have been turning off a switch?'

Virginia thought hard, but in the end she had to say 'No, I didn't. And I think I would have done because I was behind him; he said "I better go first to show the way" and so I followed behind.'

Len looked doubtful. 'There must be an alarm system,' he insisted. 'Of course knowing you were coming he could have switched it off before you arrived. You got on all right with him, did you?'

Virginia laughed. 'Very much so. He told me he wasn't quite an extinct volcano.'

'By God, that's one way of putting it.'

'There's another, smaller, room leading off from the end of the gallery.'

'More pictures?'

'I didn't go in. Yes, more pictures. But of a special kind, so the old lecher assured me. Apparently he's got a collection of pornographic stuff in there, paintings and photographs which he is very anxious to show me, so I'm going up there again soon. Next Wednesday, in fact.'

'You don't seem to have wasted your time.'

'But, Len, that isn't all. Nothing like all. Just before I left I had a wonderful idea. An absolute brainwave. I've got Bern's permission to sit in his gallery and make a copy of the van Dysen picture!'

Len stared hard at her, considering.

'You have?' he asked at last.

She nodded excitedly. 'Yes. He fell for it absolutely hook, line and sinker. I'm an art student, consumed with a passion for the Dutch school and the one thing I would like to do above all else is to make a copy of the *Woman with a Flageolet.* Incidentally I shall have to let the d.o.m. show me his collection of dirty pictures, but I'll play that as it comes along; just give him enough encouragement to keep him looking forward to the next time, because, you see, the beauty of this is that there will have to be several next times. You can't make a copy of a van Dysen in just one session. At any rate I'll take damned good care I can't. I'll be going up to Pine Place frequently and—Len—each time I'll be carrying a wrapped canvas with me and I'll carry it away each time, too, so that the security man will be absolutely used to seeing me come in and out with a parcel and won't think anything of it—what about that for an idea?'

Len grinned in genuine appreciation. 'It's a damned good idea,' he agreed, 'a damned good idea. And one day, somehow, the wrapped up canvas you are carrying will be the picture that matters eh? Is that the scheme?'

'That's it.'

'Exactly how are you going to manage that?'

'*Exactly,* I don't know yet. I've got to work that out. But the point is it will be possible.'

Len considered. 'I daresay it will,' he agreed at length, slowly. 'I daresay it will. But that's only the beginning, getting hold of the thing—'

'We can't do much if we don't get hold of it.'

'O.K. O.K. Don't get het up. You're always ready to blow your top. Comes of having these half-baked revolutionary ideas of yours I suppose. If we are going to have a scheme we've got to think it through to the end. You've hatched up what looks like a really good idea for getting hold of the picture. O.K.

Good for you. So far so good. But that's only half of it. Less than half. We've got to have somewhere to hide the picture and somewhere to hide you and presumably to get you out of the country as soon as we can. And we've got to think up some safe way of getting in touch with old man Bern and of getting hold of the money; always provided that he's willing to cough up—'

'Of course he'll cough up. He's mad about his Dutch pictures. He'll pay anything to get back *Woman with a Flageolet.*'

'Maybe he will, maybe he will. I'm only thinking things out; thinking all round it. I haven't done this sort of thing before, it isn't my line really.'

'What right has Julius Bern to own the picture anyway?'

'For Chrissake don't start that political stuff. Bern's got the dough; he wants the picture; he buys it. Pays cash down; a quarter of a million. Good luck to him. In my book he has every right to own the thing. The point is we want to take it off him. Right or wrong doesn't come into it. We want the picture and you've come up with what looks like a top-notch idea for getting hold of it. But, like I said, that means there's still a lot to be thought out and arranged; so you go ahead with your side of it and just leave me to work out the rest.'

TEN

Progress report

HOOKY WAS invited to tea in Eaton Square. Lois Chanderley got the tray ready and brought it in herself. It was Fenton's day off, she explained, and some minor disarrangement had affected the rest of the staff 'and, in any case I enjoy doing it' she said, 'the theory that any fool can make tea properly is nonsense; I may be foolish in many things but I'll back myself to make tea against anybody.'

Savouring the incredibly delicate taste of the rarest Formosa Oolong Hooky had no doubt that she would win her wager. He studied his hostess in admiration that had something of exasperation about it. What right had anyone, he wondered, to look so well-bred and elegant in the make-shift, three-ply, balsa wood world of today.

'Tell me about Ginny,' she said.

'I was able to do her a good turn at the wedding reception. She wanted to be introduced to Julius Bern and I happened to know him.'

'Julius Bern? He's one of Leo's city—I was going to say friends, *acquaintances* rather; and he must be getting on for seventy. What on earth did Ginny want to meet him for? I hope to heaven she hasn't got any designs on the old boy.'

Hooky laughed. 'I wouldn't think so. As you say he's knocking on a bit. Not that that necessarily means all his fires are extinct. But this is something quite harmless, Virginia wants to see Bern's collection of Dutch pictures.'

'Oh, I see. Yes, that makes sense. She studied art for the best part of two years; and I think she could have been quite a good artist herself if she had only stuck to it, but of course she got caught up in those wild ideas of hers.'

'At a guess I'd say she isn't doing anything particularly wild at the moment.'

'Have you found out where she's living?'

'Cleedon Court. A block of flats just off the Marylebone Road, not far from Baker Street Station.'

'That doesn't sound too slummy and sleezy.'

'It isn't.'

'Is she living alone?'

'I don't know; I haven't been asked in yet.'

Lois Chanderley smiled at her guest and said, 'I should imagine ladies often do ask you in, Mr Hefferman.'

'Only too often,' Hooky agreed, 'only too often; but so far your daughter has shown more sense. She is obviously embroiled to some extent with a man, somebody called Len'—he paused waiting for possible elucidation but Lois was unable to give him any.

'Len,' she turned the name over. 'It doesn't mean anything to me; but then I have been completely out of touch with what Ginny's doing for some time; that's what we are relying on you to tell us about. Who is this Len, have you any idea?'

'None. Yet. He's a man and Virginia is clearly keen on him; at a guess I'd say a good deal keener than he is on her.'

'Oh dear, poor Ginny; she always will go baldheaded at everything.'

'And I think she is still suffering badly from what happened to her brother in Northern Ireland.'

Lois Chanderley set her cup down carefully on the tray and looked steadily across at Hooky.

'Don't you think that we are all suffering from it, Mr Hefferman?' she asked. 'I was Alec's mother, I brought him into the world.'

Hooky nodded; the world is stuffed full of idiocies, he reflected, and by and large there's nothing much you can profitably do or say about them; he changed the subject.

'Virginia has agreed to let me take her out again,' he said, 'so I shall soon be learning how she has got on with Julius Bern, and I'll report in due course to you.'

'If this involves you in any expense—'

'None at all as yet. Being thirsty by nature I should be going to The Good Soldier in any case and if I'm lucky enough to persuade an attractive girl to come with me—*tant mieux.*'

Sir Leo had come into the room during the last few minutes and when he saw Hooky to the door he reverted to the question of expense.

'Bit tricky to talk about fees and costs between gentlemen,' he said, 'but I learnt a long time ago that there's more than one way of cooking a goose. You ever dabbled on the Stock Exchange?'

'Never. I've seldom had the money to do so for one thing and I wouldn't have the faintest idea what or when to buy for another.'

'Wise man,' Sir Leo said approvingly, 'a lot of people are walking about in the City today with the seats of their trousers hanging out just because they weren't as sensible as that. Still there's always a first time for everything. If you can scrape a few pounds together why not give your broker a ring and tell him to buy some PBP shares for you?'

'PBP?'

Sir Leo was startled by the hoot of laughter Hooky let out. 'Perry Best & Partington—Metal people,' he explained. 'What's so funny about that?'

'There's nothing funny about it,' Hooky assured him. 'I was thinking of something else for the moment. I'll do exactly as you say, Sir Leo, and thanks for the tip.'

THE GIRL who had been under discussion at tea was living in a state alternating between excitement and, occasionally, something approaching despair. This was nothing new for Virginia who never did things by halves and was accustomed, as her mother had told Hooky, to go bald-headed for anything she imagined she wanted. There was no pretence about her enjoyment in making a copy of the van Dysen. *Woman with a Flageolet* was a marvellous piece of painting; the longer Virginia sat opposite to it, patiently studying every tiny detail, every trick and artifice that the artist had used to get his effects, the more she realised what a genius the man was.

She worked slowly, sometimes studying the original closely for ten minutes together before putting a single further touch to what she knew already was going to be a hopelessly inadequate copy.

All this was perfectly genuine; but there was another reason for not hurrying. Len, who at her first mention of it had been so much in favour of her scheme now seemed to have lost something of his keenness. The more he seemed inclined to waver the more Virginia was determined to succeed; if Len doubted, Len must be convinced; especially with that god-damned red-head knocking around... *I'm not going to rush this* Virginia told herself, *I'll take it gently. I'll get everybody at Pine Place so used to my coming and going that they'll accept me as a normal part of the set-up...*

So it was established that she went there on two afternoons a week—*come every day if you want to,* Bern urged, *and stay as long as you like; it does an old man like me good to have such a charming companion, it reminds me of my youth...*

Virginia smiled at that, but rationed herself to two visits a week. She left her canvas and easel in position in the gallery at the end of each copying session, but she took care always to be carrying a fair sized flat parcel whenever she came to or left Pine Place. Julius Bern seldom saw her actual arrival and hardly realised the fact that she was invariably carrying something; Goddard and Lessing, having been warned that the visitor was an artist, saw nothing strange in the fact that she never appeared without something the size and shape of a wrapped up picture under her arm.

By now Virginia had established the friendliest of relations with Goddard, and in order to further herself in his good books, had even managed to look as though she enjoyed talking to Zena the Alsatian bitch. The security man, who genuinely loved his dog, approved of this.

'Zena likes you, Miss. I can tell that. She's all right with anyone she takes a fancy to, anyone as I tell her is O.K.; but if there was anybody who ought not to be here and I told her *see 'em off*—oh my word!...'

'Don't tell her to see me off, Mr Goddard, will you?'

'Not likely, Miss. Mrs Goddard was saying to me only yesterday it's a good thing the old gentleman has got a friend coming to see him regularly.'

'How is Mrs Goddard's back?'

The state of his wife's back was one of the staple constituents of Goddard's conversation and a subject which he was always ready to discuss; that Virginia should remember to enquire about it confirmed his opinion that she was very much an 'all right' person; in reply to her diplomatic query he made the remarkable answer, 'Well it comes and goes, Miss; you know how these things are.'

Virginia nodded sympathetically.

She had not been able to establish quite such friendly relations with Lessing; it was not that the manservant had the slightest suspicion of her real motive in coming to Pine Place but simply that he was influenced by Mrs Lessing who, like many people who have never had the opportunity or courage to flout the moral code, managed to work herself up into a fine indignation about anyone else who did.

'A young woman of twenty-three or four and an old man of seventy—I call it disgusting.'

'She comes here to copy this picture he bought recently.'

'I'm sure she does—and what else I wonder?'

'Miss Cave's an artist, Ada.'

'We all know what that means! What about that little room at the end of the gallery and what's in there?'

'That's nothing to do with us, Ada.'

'Well, p'raps it isn't. But all the same we know what he's got hidden away in there, don't we? All I can say is for a man to take a girl in there and look at those pictures and photographs with her—well!'

'It's not for us—' Lessing began sententiously only to be cut short by his wife's 'Don't come any of your *Upstairs Downstairs* stuff on me, Albert. Where would the old gentleman be if we weren't here to look after him?'

'He'd be here in Pine Place, looked after by somebody else; and you and I might be anywhere; but it wouldn't be as good a job as this. Or half as good. And you know it.'

Virginia had been twice with Bern into the little room at the end of the gallery. Each time he produced a key from his pocket and smiled at her as he opened the door. 'Quite a number of people come to see my Dutch pictures,' he said, 'but they don't all get asked in here; not by any means, my dear.'

Inside Virginia had found exactly what she had expected to find, only perhaps on a more exuberant and exotic scale; Bern must have ransacked the sex shops of Europe to get stuff like this, she thought; where on earth did he find it? Germany? Scandinavia?

For the first few minutes she was fascinated; but the fascination of curiosity soon became boredom not far removed from revulsion. Like most full-of-life young people who can get intense pleasure out of the art of love-making, Virginia found very little pleasure, and indeed something more like old-fashioned embarrassment, in looking at pictures and photographs of people paid to pose in the act and in grotesque distortions of it. As they went slowly round the extraordinary display Bern kept close to her side; when he halted to call her attention to one particular outrageous fantasy he stood very close behind her indeed. She could feel him pressed up against her and was aware of his quickened breathing...

'They're rather amusing aren't they?' he asked.

'Fantastic.'

'I sometimes walk round looking at them without my clothes on.'

'Julius, you're a naughty old man.'

Virginia reported all this in Len's flat. Len was sitting in his shirt sleeves disgruntled because England was playing Portugal in a World Cup match and the T.V. had broken down.

'Just when there's something worth seeing,' he grumbled. 'Any other evening, if one of these fatuous comics was on, or some god-damned politician telling us just tighten your belt a bit more and remember Dunkirk and vote for me and everything in the garden will be lovely, the bloody set would be working perfectly, but this evening, of course not. How are you getting on then?'

Virginia told him about her visit to the little private room. 'It's exactly what I thought, Len; he's got a collection of dirty pictures in there and he gets his kicks looking at them; it's probably the only way he can get kicks now.'

'Has he tried anything with you?'

'He told me he likes to have a girl with him when he goes round.'

Being deprived of his England v. Portugal game had put Len in a bad mood and he said sharply, 'Well, apart from the fact that you are getting a good show of porn how much further on are we?'

Virginia laughed. 'A whole lot,' she told him. 'I've got the thing worked out now. I see how it can be done. Julius keeps that little private sex-show of his locked. I don't blame him; he says he fairly often has friends who come to look at the Dutch pictures and he doesn't want them going any further. I've been in there twice with him now. Each time he produces a key from his pocket and unlocks the door. And, Len, listen, whilst we are going round looking at the porn he leaves the key in the door and he locks it again when we come out.'

'So?'

'Well, it's too easy isn't it? I go in with him to the little room; when he's in the middle of getting his kicks from one of the photographs I suddenly make a bolt for it, dart outside, slam the door to and lock it. Then I lift the van Dysen off the wall, wrap it in brown paper so that it looks exactly like the parcel I've been carrying every day I've been up to Pine Place and walk straight out with it. You can have the car handy in Acacia Road and there we are!'

Len considered this in gloomy silence for a while and then asked, 'And what's happened to Bern's voice? Has he gone dumb or something? Doesn't he start shouting?'

'Of course he'll shout, but the room hasn't got any windows and it's tucked away right up in a corner of the house, miles away from the kitchen quarters. With any luck he could be there half an hour, and longer, before anybody heard anything.'

'And you reckon you could get past the security man in the garden?'

'I'm sure I could. Goddard and I are friends now. Buddies. I ask after his wife's back every time I see him. He's completely used to my going in and out carrying a wrapped up canvas under my arm; he won't suspect a thing.'

Len thought again for a moment, then said, 'How big is this Woman with the what-you-may-call it?'

'Sixty-two by forty-five.'

'Sixty-two by forty-five what? Feet? Yards?'

'For God's sake, Len. I know you're in a bad temper because you can't see the damned football match, but try not to be too silly. Centimetres, of course, it's the way they talk about pictures.'

'What's it mean in feet and inches?'

'Twenty-five inches by eighteen. Two foot one by a foot and a half. I can carry it easily.'

'I suppose you could.'

'It's a pretty easy way of getting hold of a quarter of a million pounds' worth of picture.'

'And what about the alarm system?'

'I've told you about that. Bern always comes with me to the gallery to see that my easel and so on is all right, and every time, every single time, the last thing he does before we go out of his study is to lift that mirror off the wall and lay it down somewhere. My guess is that taking the weight of the mirror off its hook disconnects the alarm system and once it's off you can open the door of the gallery without any warning being given to anybody.'

Len nodded and said, 'Sounds likely,' and Virginia gave an angry little laugh.

'You're not exactly enthusiastic are you?' she said.

'Keep the volume down, chick, don't get excited. I've never been a bull-at-a-gate man and I'm not going to start now. You've worked your bit out splendidly. Full marks for that. But I've told you already getting hold of the picture is only one half of it. It's got to be hidden, and so have you; and there's got to be some system of getting in touch with Bern about the ransom money. You don't suppose the Law will be sitting on its arse doing nothing all this time, do you? They'll be buzzing around like bloody bluebottles. I've got a lot of thinking to do on this, and I'm not going to do it this evening. I've other things to do.'

'Other people to see, you mean.'

Len lit a cigarette and flicked away the spent match. 'All right then, if you want to hear me say it, somebody else to see.'

'And curiously enough so have I,' Virginia retorted. 'You don't imagine I mope up there by myself all the time wondering what you are doing when that damned little red car of hers is parked outside do you?'

ELEVEN

Poisoning the wells

'WHAT'S HAPPENING to Len Carron these days?' the underworld wondered.

'Woman trouble.'

'Woman trouble? Len? Never. He lays 'em and leaves 'em. No problem.'

'This one's a bit of a problem apparently. A redhead called Stella.'

Len himself was not quite sure how his relations with Stella had become what they were. At the outset he hadn't wanted, and certainly hadn't intended, to get so much caught up with her. His boast to Virginia about being a loner had been perfectly genuine at the time. His feelings about Virginia herself had been genuine too, or as nearly genuine as he was in the habit of letting his feelings be. He had liked the look of her when he first saw her on the staircase of Roddy Marten's flat. She looked as though she had breeding and guts and Len Carron admired both those things. He had been intrigued to find out who she was, and had been amused, in a tolerant way, for what he thought of as her juvenile revolutionary ideas. She had shown him how right he was about breeding and guts in the abortive wages-snatch; it certainly hadn't been her fault that things had gone wrong there. Len was flattered that she had evidently gone overboard for him; she had given the fatuous Roddy Marten the go-by without a moment's hesitation and now he knew perfectly well that if he crooked his little finger she would come hurrying down at any time from the top-floor flat.

It looked like an ideal set-up, but Len had learnt to mistrust ideal set-ups. Fate doesn't seem to like them. Just when everything looks settled and O.K. Fate explodes a land mine.

The land mine in Len Carron's case had been Stella.

Stella was short, smart and for all her superficial femininity harder than most nails. Len himself didn't know why she had hit him twixt wind and water; if he gave his mind to it he could list several things about her which he actively disliked, and yet—how the hell could you dislike half a person and yet find you couldn't do without the other half he wondered...

She sat opposite him now, in the small living room of his flat, a length of leg showing beneath a very short skirt.

Glass in hand she studied him. 'You don't drink enough, Len.'

'I have a drink when I want to.'

'Well, want to now—keep me company.'

After a moment's hesitation Carron mixed himself a whisky and soda, the woman watched him, secretly amused at her little triumph.

She raised her glass. 'Cheers. How's that little card-carrying friend of yours?' she asked.

'Who says she's card-carrying?'

'Well, if she isn't she ought to be. She calls herself an actress doesn't she? A member of Equity I suppose and God knows that's stuffed full of little Trots. Honestly, Len, they make me sick. Why can't they get on with their job and leave all this political stuff alone?'

'I'm not interested in her political ideas.'

'You will be, though, if she has anything to do with it. These Lefties are like the R.C.s, always trying to talk you round to their way of thinking. She'll convert you, Len.'

'Like hell she will.'

Stella laughed; it always amused her to rile him. She had heard Len describe himself as a 'loner'... that's as may be, she had thought; she herself could improve on that; she coined a phrase for herself *I'm a oner,* and she knew that it exactly expressed how she wanted things to be. She wanted Len for herself; she couldn't stand the idea of a rival; any rival, actual or potential, would have to be got rid of.

'Why do you suppose she does it, Len?'

'Does what?'

'What I mean is—a house in Eaton Square and plenty of money in the family, why go in for all this political nonsense—always assuming that it's genuine, of course.'

'I've told you I'm not interested in her political games; and what's all this about *genuine?* Why shouldn't she be genuine?'

'I'm just saying *if* she's genuine; *if;* that's all. And anyway she's interested in someone else, isn't she?'

'What are you talking about now?'

'I saw her get out of a fellow's car outside the flat here only yesterday.'

'Did he come in?'

'No he didn't. Not this time anyway. They stood talking for a minute or two then he got back into his car and drove off.'

'What the hell are you bleating about then? And anyway she's come up with a first-class scheme for getting hold of that picture.'

'Are you becoming an art collector or something?'

'For God's sake don't start being sarcastic. That picture was bought for a quarter of a million in Christie's not so long ago; a quarter of a million! That's a hell of a lot of money.'

'I like to hear you talk about cash, Len; when it's cash you're on your proper pitch, you mean what you say. A picture isn't cash, Len.'

'Bern will pay ransom for it.'

'Are you sure?'

'Virginia says he will.'

'Oh well, that settles it, of course. Anything she says must be right. Be your age, Len. This ransom business isn't your line, anyway; you told me that yourself, didn't you?'

'I may have done.'

'And what's she going up to St John's Wood three times a week for?'

'That's all part of the plan, she's got to get to know Bern—'

'I should think she knows him pretty well by now, doesn't she? I expect it's all right, Len; you always know best; I just wonder what her little game really is, that's all—'

'What do you mean? Little game? She hasn't got a little game.'

Stella held out her glass to be refilled and said her final word, 'Of course she hasn't, Len—not if she's genuine.'

'HEFFERMAN calling.'

'Who?'

'Hefferman; even in Eton days referred to as Hooky. Remember me?'

'Only too well.'

'Remember what a perfectly horrible little boy you were and what a kind and considerate fag master I made?'

'I never knew you had such a powerful imagination, Hooky.'

'How's the world with you, Nick? Rumour has it that you're one of the big shots on the Stock Exchange these days.'

'If you believe that you'll believe anything; but I'm getting by.'

'Like to do a bit of business for me?'

'I never turn down business; what is it?'

'By a series of miracles I have scraped together two hundred and fifty quid. I want you to buy me two hundred and fifty quid's worth of PBP shares.'

'Come again.'

'PBP.'

'I thought you said that, but I couldn't believe you meant it. Perry Best & Partington you're talking about, is that right?'

'Those are the boys. Two hundred and fifty quid's worth of 'em.'

'You want your head examined, Hooky, which doesn't surprise me remembering what you were like at Eton. Nobody's asked me to buy any PBP for months and months. They're on the floor. Whatever makes you pick on them?'

'When the mouth of the horse opens and words emerge the wise man pays attention. Chu Ling.'

'Chu who?'

'Ling. One of the financial advisers to the Celestial Empire.'

'Well, if he's advising you to buy PBP he's off his celestial rocker.'

'Nevertheless I propose to follow his advice.'

'You always were a pig-headed sort of a devil. However, as you say. After all, you're the client; if you want to throw away two hundred and fifty smackers who am I to try and stop you? Wait whilst I get the sheet—here we are, PBP quoted today at seven p. I should think they have stood at that figure for the past twelve months and are highly unlikely to go above it for the next twelve.'

'Seven p? Then I'll get a lot of shares for my two fifty won't I?'

'Quite a lot. And good luck to you, chum; only don't say I didn't warn you.'

Hooky was finding the mission he had undertaken for Leo and Lois Chanderley mildly frustrating. Nothing much was coming of it either one way or the other. If Virginia preferred to live away from her family that, in Hooky's opinion, was her affair;

and he had certainly not been able to report anything particularly alarming about the sort of life she seemed to be leading. So far no drugs, orgies or demonstrations; all her interest at the moment seemed to be centred on her visits to Pine Place and the apparently absorbing business of copying Julius Bern's latest acquisition.

Hooky was quite prepared to believe that having an attractive girl of twenty-four in the house might tempt Bern to try a few elderly masculine gambits, but he felt perfectly certain that Virginia could handle any trouble in that line, the more so since he himself had made astonishingly little progress on the personal front.

He was used to getting a pretty lively response in his dealings with women and in his candid moments he had to admit that it irked him slightly to have made so little impression on Virginia; they had been together to The Good Soldier four times in all now, and each time he found that his first assessment of her as 'prickly' was confirmed. Virginia gave as good as she got in conversation, which made her fun to talk to; and when, as occasionally happened, she lapsed into something more serious and with a personal note in it—as for instance when she spoke about her soldier brother's death in Northern Ireland—Hooky felt he might be getting somewhere, but these interludes were brief and never came to anything. Then there was 'Len'; Len was mentioned fairly often, but only in quick, passing references. Len was never dilated upon or explained. Tentative queries about Len were met with the brush-off direct *mind your own business*—excellent advice as Hooky himself was bound to admit, and had he followed it throughout his life he would have avoided a lot of trouble and missed a lot of fun.

Len was evidently the current man in the girl's life and, like all current affairs that Hooky had ever known, this one seemed to consist of a series of crises. Hooky had a suspicion that Virginia was busily making a complete hash of the affair with Len; and he was beginning to form the opinion that she was the sort of girl destined to make a complete hash of any love affair. Were they actually living together in the flat in Cleedon Court? Hooky didn't know. He had not yet been inside Cleedon Court; he had been allowed to run Virginia back there from The Good Soldier but it had been a case of thus far and no further.

'Don't I get asked in?' he queried.

'What do you want to come in for?'

'I have immoral longings in me, like somebody or other in Shakespeare.'

'Cleopatra actually, and you've misquoted her to suit your own ends. Just like a man.'

'My God, you women's libbers never let up do you?'

'Thanks for the evening, I enjoyed it.'

'Go your own sweet way.'

'I have every intention of doing so.'

'And if you do get in a jam of any sort come to Uncle Hooky, the old reliable firm.'

'Old, or at least ageing certainly,' Virginia said cruelly; 'but reliable? I'm not so sure about that.'

But there were moments, especially when she was racked with jealousy, and desperately wanted somebody to confide in, somebody to whom she could explain what a perfectly bloody thing it was to be mad about a man who didn't really fundamentally give a damn for you, who would much sooner have his red-headed little bitch—these were the moments when Virginia was tempted to think that she might take Hooky at his word and turn to him if not for advice and help at least for an audience, at least for an ear; at least for somebody to unburden herself to; he was, after all, a man, he might in some extremity of disillusionment be somebody to make a fool of oneself with, to try to forget things with . . .

HOOKY WALKED into the saloon bar of The Good Soldier unaccompanied. The clock said seven. Vodka time. The hour of rehabilitation from the buffets of the day. The hour of illusion. The hour of make-believe; the hour when, for a space, it was possible to forget that people were shooting one another on strictly religious grounds in Ireland, blowing one another up for fun in the Lebanon or just quietly dying of starvation in the streets of Calcutta.

'Sir is without Madam?' Cyril greeted him archly.

'On my tod,' Hooky agreed.

It was too early for The Good Soldier to be busy and there were in fact only two other people in the bar—a woman whom Hooky did not know and a man whom he instantly recognised, an ardent pilgrim worshipping at the shrine.

'Hallo Prof,' Hooky greeted him. 'What brings you here? How's tricks? How are things on the philosophical front?'

Doctor Stuart-Crawley turned in delight.

'My dear sir,' he exclaimed. 'What an agreeable surprise. Now, let me try to remember; don't tell me; my memory a somewhat unreliable faculty when floundering in the doldrums of sobriety, functions splendidly when activated by alcohol—ah, I have it: Hove, The Wheatsheaf and Mrs Drew. My God. What a woman! Beware of women, my dear sir; if I remember rightly there was an aunt looming menacingly in your background. Most women are menacing—this lady will excuse me, I'm sure for saying such an outrageous thing—'

The lady smiled encouragingly at him; she didn't know the old oddity from a crow; but he had the excuse of being stewed to the gills; and he had insisted on 'being in the chair', he was paying for her drinks; so naturally she smiled. She was there on her own only because the man she was interested in was out of London for the evening and had told her he would not be back till late.

'—now Cyril is much more amenable. Cyril and I have already established a *rapport* haven't we, Cyril?'

'If you say so, Doctor.'

'Don't tell me your name,' the Professor continued, 'because in due course I shall remember it and everything about you. Just tell Cyril what you would like to drink and please allow me to pay for it. I am in funds. Dame fortune has smiled upon me, something that withered hag seldom does.'

'School mastering is doing well then?' Hooky hazarded.

The Professor winced. 'Pray don't remind me so lightheartedly of my drudgery,' he begged. 'Yet when I say drudgery it is drudgery, I must admit, enlivened by passages of delight. Cherubic little boys; chubby, cheeky and so eminently smackable. Little horrors, of course, the apples, no doubt, of their mothers' eyes and crammed to the brim with every sort of dishonesty and iniquity; leaders of industry and cabinet ministers in the making. Cyril, you are neglecting our glasses—'

'I was interested in what you were saying, Doctor.'

'All my life I have constantly let the will o' the wisp of pleasure distract me from the stern path of duty. I strongly advise you not to follow my example; what we now require is a large gin and tonic for this lady who listens with such flattering interest to the ramblings of an alcoholic intellectual; a Pimm's Number One for my powerful looking friend; and my own usual innocuous mixture.'

'Just as you say, Doctor.'

The double brandy laced with vodka which Cyril poured out didn't look to Hooky like an innocuous mixture; it looked lethal. It was clear that the Professor was flying high, wide and handsome. Over his freshly charged glass Hooky winked at the woman perched on the third stool at the bar; he had no idea who she was, but if she stuck around for a while she was obviously going to get a large number of free drinks; it was going to be one of those evenings...

The woman didn't return his wink; she had seen this man before and she was searching her memory to make quite certain of the occasion...

Hooky had come to The Good Soldier on the off chance that Virginia might look in there; such a lucky meeting had happened before and Hooky, ever an optimist, had hopes that it might occur again. As the minutes ticked away his hopes began to fade, but meanwhile there was always the Professor...

'I am dismayed,' that worthy man was saying, 'that you have not asked what occasions my appearance in this monstrous wen of London, but as you have failed to do so I am obliged to volunteer the information and to tell you that I can now call myself *author;* I am about to have a book published.'

Hooky was tempted to respond *'Who isn't?'*, but he had no wish to shoot down the bright bird of happiness in full flight so he substituted 'Good on you, Prof. Written a masterpiece have you?'

'I have written nothing. As yet. It may be true that authors are the natural prey of publishers; but not always. Today—I think it was today, but Cyril's ministrations are blurring the sharp edges of memory somewhat; but, yes, it was today that I lunched—at his expense, mark you—with a youth of high ideals and, I am delighted to say, of extreme gullibility, the scales not yet fallen from his eyes. In me he beheld not, as he should have done, a rose-red cissy half as old as time, but, God be praised, a distinguished art historian, capable, as I convinced him after the second bottle of really excellent Burgundy (he had the good sense not only to pay for the wine but also to let me choose it) capable of writing for him exactly the prestigious—God Almighty, what a dreadful word, but this callow youth used it, he would go far in that factory of distorted English, the BBC—I am in the middle, my muscular friend, of telling you something of high importance but for the moment it has slipped my memory—'

'It sounds to me as though you've got a contract to write a book,' Hooky said.

The Professor was delighted with the prompt. *'Rem acu tetigisti,'* he cried, 'and we all remember enough of our Latin to know what that means. My dear Hefferman—I remember your name now and not only your name but your sobriquet, my dear Hooky, you are bang on target. Slightly fuddled by the admirable Burgundy and completely engulfed by a spate of high-flown nonsense from myself this fledgling publisher has given me a contract to write for him a book called—I thought it up between the bottles of Burgundy—*Art Criticism of the West seen in Historical Perspective,* can you imagine a more fatuous title? It will take me a long time to work out what it means; if indeed it means anything. But it turned the trick. These young intellectuals with University damp still behind their ears love that sort of jargon. Of course the contract, *per se,* was nothing. A fig for your contract. Except that a lady is present and that Cyril's ears are, I am afraid, innocent I would describe a suitable course of action with the contract. But the contract contained amongst much legal nonsense about dates of delivery and so on, to which I shall pay no attention, the blessed words *on signature.* I signed the silly document this afternoon in the innocent babe's office and, *on signature,* I was given a cheque for two hundred and fifty pounds. Our glasses. Cyril, stand empty; why, when there is such good fortune to celebrate?'

'I was listening to what you were saying, Professor.'

'May I point out that standing and waiting is not enough? People who do that are also expected to serve; kindly get on with it.'

Hooky stayed the course manfully for well over an hour but he then withdrew. He could recognise a better man when he saw him, and this Ph.D. merchant, who liberally sprinkled his talk with Latin tags and occasionally even strayed exuberantly into Greek, had obviously got hollow legs and a cast-iron head. The Prof was a very notable imbiber; Hooky had not kept an exact account of the number of double brandies and vodka that went to lubricate that fluent tongue but it was formidable; 'I'm off to dine with some nobs in Eaton Square,' he announced and he was glad to find himself outside in Grafton Street still more or less in his right mind and in good order.

Inside The Good Soldier the red-headed woman who had not done badly in the gin-and-tonic line was also preparing to leave. She didn't see much to interest her either in the Professor—who seemed to her to be a nutcase—or in Cyril. She disliked their sort almost as much as Len did. But before going she had a question to ask. She knew now where she had previously seen the man who had just left. She had seen him in the driving seat of a car outside Cleedon Court. A car out of which Len's other current interest, the little Trotskyite from Equity, had climbed.

If this was the little Trot's boy friend Stella wanted to learn all she could about him.

'Who's your friend Professor?' she asked.

Doctor Stuart-Crawley declared in passionate tones that Cyril was his friend.

'But apart from all that—the man who just went out, the chunky looking chap, who is he?'

The Professor looked solemn and dropped his voice a semitone.

'That man,' he said, 'is a Private Investigator.'

Stella was startled. It was true that this bird practically had vodka running out of his ears but he gave no signs of being non compos.

'He is?'

'What I believe in fiction is known as a Private Eye.'

'Are you sure about this? Certain?'

'Oh, what a dusty answer gets the soul when hot from certainties in this our life. Certain? Yes, I am as certain as I can be. He told me so himself. Confidential missions undertaken. Private investigations carried out. Villains and lawbreakers brought to book, an invaluable member of a civilisation in decay; you are not going, my dear lady, are you?'

'Yes I am. I must.'

'You leave Cyril and me to console one another.'

'I expect you'll manage,' Stella said.

TWELVE

'You're being taken for a ride'

LEN HAD been to St Albans, where in a modest house in a law-abiding crescent there lived a man who had once—like Len himself—seen the inside of Durham jail and who knew more than most about the ways and means of hiding people or objects the Law wanted to find.

The St Albans visit had gone without a hitch and Len found himself back in London much earlier than he had expected to be. 'I shan't be back till late,' he had told Stella, but as things had turned out here he was getting ready to let himself into the flat a full two hours before he had expected.

Len was pleased that the St Albans arrangements had all gone so smoothly but annoyed to find himself unexpectedly at a loose end; he was now regretting what he had told Stella. As he was getting out his keys Virginia came in through the street door of the block of flats and began to walk towards the lift.

Len's own front door was in a darkened corner of the entrance hall and for a moment Virginia was unaware that he was standing there. He called out to her, and her head jerked up in surprise. These days she was half eager, half defensive about Len. In self-protection she told herself that as far as she was concerned Len Carron was just like any other man; she could take him or leave him. All lies, of course; Len wasn't just like any other man and the thought that the hard-as-nails little red-head had got much closer to him than she herself had was torture.

'Hallo there,' he called.

She was in slight confusion for a moment. 'Sorry. I didn't see you.'

'Come in for a drink—'

Virginia began to walk slowly towards him. 'I'd like to come in,' she said.

Len smiled at her; he had thought she was attractive the very first time he had caught sight of her outside Roddy Marten's flat, he had thought so again when he had seen her on the stage of the Haymarket; he still thought she was attractive; but of course Stella had come on the scene since then and, he had to admit it, Stella had knocked him sideways; Stella had managed to get under his skin to a much greater degree than he usually permitted a woman to do; but that didn't alter the fact that Virginia had a lot about her that appealed to him and in any case she was proving herself an invaluable partner. There was the additional circumstance that at the moment, and rather an empty loose-end moment at that, Stella wasn't on hand and Virginia was.

'How are things going?' he asked when they were in the flat.

'I've been wondering when you would ask. I suppose you've been too busy.' (It wasn't what she really wanted to say but, being Virginia, it was what, in fact, she *did* say.)

Len laughed easily; he wanted to talk to her and he wasn't going to let her rile him.

'Up at Pine Place,' he prompted. 'Everything O.K.?'

'Yes. Fine. In a way. But I can't go on copying the van Dysen for ever; the old boy may begin to wonder a bit. Actually I don't suppose he will because of course he thinks I go up there for other things as well which incidentally I hate.'

'A nuisance is he?'

'Oh God Len, all this fumbling, furtive old man stuff—beastly.'

'He's got quite a collection of porn hasn't he?'

'Go up and ask him to show it to you if you are keen. I'm not going to talk about it. Making love is one thing; looking at pictures of other people's variations on it is something else and I'm simply not interested, but of course I have to pretend that I am to keep Julius Bern sweet.'

'Well, it won't be for much longer now; I'm just back from fixing up a place where you and the picture can hide out for a day or two before we get you out of the country.'

'Where?'

'St Albans.'

'St Albans? Why on earth do I have to go there?'

'Never mind "why". Just get that picture out safely, that's your part of the job. And, incidentally, when you get to St Albans do as you're told. Exactly. None of your wild stuff.'

'You do like issuing orders, don't you?'

Len gave a hard, dry laugh. 'You can't get anywhere without orders,' he said. 'It may sound funny to you but I'm a great believer in law and order. I'm a villain and I want society organised so that I can pursue my villainy in peace—none of these demonstrations and sit-ins and squat-downs and all the rest of the nonsense that you militant lot go in for. The man at St Albans is called Chalky. There isn't the slightest reason why the law should connect him with our little coup and when it comes to hiding people or things he knows it all. Only, like I just said, do as he tells you.'

'How long shall I have to be there?'

'God knows. He'll fix you up abroad as soon as he can. It depends how the game goes. The law doesn't give up easily, you know; the bastards have got records and files and once they get started on a case they're apt to keep on at it. You thought this scheme up, remember; you're not chickening out on it are you?'

'Of course I'm not chickening out, damn you.'

'O.K., O.K., don't get steamed up. Actually I could understand if you did want to throw your hand in. I'm a villain because that's the way life went for me from the start, but anyone with your background and upbringing, well I can't understand why you want to get mixed up with this sort of thing at all—the money?'

'I rather despise money.'

Len laughed. 'By God, I don't. That's dewy-eyed nonsense if ever I heard any. You only say that, Chickie, because you were brought up with plenty of the stuff behind you. You just do it for the kicks, then, do you?'

'Partly.'

Len lit a cigarette, inhaled a lungful of smoke and slowly expelled it before saying thoughtfully, 'Of course you could be a plant. One of these agent's provocateurs.' (Stella's '*... if she's genuine*' had suddenly pushed itself into his consciousness.)

'That's me,' Virginia said gaily. 'The *femme fatale* luring you to your doom. You don't seriously think that, Len, do you? How could you? Unless somebody has been putting ideas in your head about me?'

Len shook his head slowly. 'No, as a matter of fact I don't think it. But I'll tell you one thing, this honour amongst thieves business that people talk about—there isn't any. Villains don't trust one another, they just hope for the best.'

'You can trust me, Len.'

'Maybe I can. Maybe you are genuine. You deliver the picture to me in the car outside Bern's house and I'll know you're genuine.'

'Don't worry, I'll bring it to you. What's going to happen to it ultimately?'

'Julius Bern is going to pay a lot of lovely money to get it back—we hope. And incidentally he may not bring the Law in at all. When you lift the picture you are going to leave a note behind telling him how much money we want and how he has got to let us have it and warning him that if he makes the slightest move to contact the police the picture will be destroyed.'

'I don't want that to happen.'

'I don't want it to happen either. What I want is thirty thousand pounds in used notes from Bern.'

'The van Dysen is worth much more than that.'

'Of course it's worth much more—didn't Bern give a quarter of a million for it? The psychology of the thing is to ask just the right price; from Bern's point of view, with all the money he has got, is it worth all the fuss and bother of getting the police in and having the Press people and interviews and the whole publicity razzamatazz simply to save himself thirty thousand quid? My guess is that he'll see the sense of coming quietly; he'll pay up and be glad to get his picture back.'

'It would be criminal to destroy a van Dysen.'

Len laughed loud and long at that. 'You're taking part in a criminal activity,' he pointed out, 'or perhaps you hadn't noticed?'

Virginia flushed and said, 'There are different sorts of crimes.'

'Too right there are. I wouldn't have touched half the people in Durham with a barge-pole. And when do we pull off our own particular bit of villainy? Now that I've got the hideout fixed up when do you reckon you can lift the picture?'

Virginia thought for a few seconds and then answered, 'A Wednesday is probably the best day. Lessing, the manservant cleans the silver on a Wednesday afternoon. That means he's occupied in his pantry and is less likely than ever to hear any shouting that may be going on when I lock Bern up in that porn gallery of his.'

'Next Wednesday then, today week?'

Virginia nodded.

'Good girl. O.K. I'll let Chalky know and I'll work out the exact time table and all the details about the getaway car and so on.'

'And whilst I'm lying low at St Albans what will you be doing, Len?'

'What will I be doing? Living a peaceful life here like the law-abiding citizen I am. If the Law does come to take a look at me I shall welcome them. They can turn this place over as often as they like and good luck to them, they'll find sweet-fanny-adams here.'

'You'll be living here all on your own?'

'I'll be living here, Chickie; and of course I shall be on my own, if I feel that way. I'm a loner, haven't I told you that already?'

'Yes, you've told me.'

The bell rang and Len looked up in surprise. 'Who the heck is that?' he said; when he went to the door and opened it Stella walked in. She had come to the flat on the chance that Len might just be back from St Albans; from her first quick glance at the scene she got the impression that he had been back for some time.

'I'm so sorry if I'm interrupting anything,' she said in her best sarcastic tones.

Len smiled sourly... *serves you right,* he told himself, *for getting mixed up with two of 'em; one's trouble enough, especially this red-headed bitch, but two of them, and fighting amongst themselves!*...

Virginia, getting up from her perch on the arm of a chair, said, 'You're not interrupting anything. I'm just on my way out.' She didn't look at Len as she made her way to the door. He got to his feet and opened the door for her, a courtesy he had never shown before. 'Be seeing you,' he said amiably; Virginia didn't appear to hear him...

Len seated himself in his chair again, threw a leg over one arm of it and stared hard at Stella. She stared just as hard back at him.

'So now you're pleased with yourself I suppose?' he said at length.

'I thought you were going to St Albans.'

'I've been to St Albans.'

'You said you wouldn't be back till late.'

'That's what I thought, but everything went well; no snags; and just for once there was hardly any traffic on the road so I got back early—what is this? A ruddy investigation or something?'

'It was very fortunate you found her here, wasn't it?'

Len paused before answering and when he spoke it was in a lower tone than usual and his words came in a slow, measured way—always a danger signal with him.

'Well, yes, if you want to know, it *was* very fortunate. Virginia and I had a very useful little chat.'

'I'll bet you did.'

'You're asking for it, you know.'

'Len, I wouldn't have believed you could be such a sucker. You're being taken for a ride.'

'What the hell are you talking about now?'

'Give me a cigarette will you?'

'Look, Stella, if you go on like this, with all this cut-the-other-girl's-throat stuff I'll give you a hell of a lot more than a cigarette I promise you.' He drew a packet of Stuyvesants out of his pocket and threw it on to a side table. 'If you want a smoke help yourself but for God's sake stop this bitching.'

Stella took a cigarette, lit it and put the neat little lighter away in her bag. She blew out a plume of smoke.

'I suppose you know that your precious Virginia has a boy friend?' she said.

'I don't expect her to act like a nun.'

'I'm sure you don't. But this evening, in The Good Soldier, I found out something interesting about that boy friend of hers.'

'Such as?'

'He's a private eye.'

Len studied that sharp, hard little face for a full thirty seconds before speaking . . . more bitching? he wondered; it was possible, of course, get two women at odds with one another over a man and any god-damned thing was possible; but somehow he didn't think that this was just a case of more bitching; he had a feeling that Stella was speaking the truth; and he didn't like the words *private eye,* they scared him a little.

'So what exactly happened in the pub?' he asked at length.

Stella told him what happened in the pub '. . . I recognised this big chap with the broken nose, I'd seen Virginia Cave get out of his car outside the flats one night, so when he went I asked the other character, who obviously knew him, who he was.'

'Who was this other character?'

'A lush—well, he ought to be anyway judging by the number of double brandies and vodka he kept lapping up, not that they seemed to make any difference to him. A professor of some sort apparently; and he sounded like it, spouting out all kinds of stuff. Latin and God knows what.'

'Sounds as though he was off his rocker.'

'Not on your life, Len; a bit odd I'll grant you but this old bird isn't off his rocker; if you ask me he's all there, he's pretty sharp. A homo like most of these intellectuals.'

'He would be.'

'But that doesn't make him a fool, Len; and when I asked him about the man who had just gone out he told me at once—he's a private investigator, confidential missions and enquiries and all that. Doesn't that girl come from one of the posh houses in Eaton Square?'

'That's where her family live. Why?'

'That's where this private eye man in the pub said he was going. *I'm off to dine with the nobs in Eaton Square,* he said.'

Len stared at her in disquiet.

'Are you making this up?' he asked, 'because if you are, by Christ, I'll trim you up good and proper.'

'Don't be silly, Len. I'm not making anything up. I don't make things up with you. With you and me it's real, genuine. I'm not the one who makes things up.'

'And this private eye merchant was going to dinner in Eaton Square?'

'That's what he said. But perhaps you think he was making that up?'

Len ignored the sharpness of her tone; he now thought that what she was telling him was true, and if it was true she was entitled to be a little sharp.

'This wants thinking out a bit,' he said.

'You're dead right there, Len.'

'I don't like this, not one little bit I don't. What was he going to Eaton Square for do you suppose?'

'To report on how things are going, presumably. The Eaton Square lot must have hired him to keep an eye on her and see she doesn't come to any harm in what she's doing.'

'And what is she doing exactly, do you reckon?'

'She's in this for kicks, Len. She must be. She's got all the money she wants; she's in it for the excitement and fun of it.'

'Fun of what exactly?'

'Acting for the police; being a nark.'

'A nark?'

'Christ, Len, you can be simple sometimes can't you? Especially if a girl waves her legs at you.'

'She wasn't doing anything for the police in the wages snatch I told you about.'

'But it didn't come off did it? You hadn't actually committed any crime when the thing blew up on you. If it had come off, things might have turned out very differently; she might have sprung a surprise on you then, don't you think?'

Len remained silent for some seconds and finally said, 'Damn it, I'd never have thought it, never.'

'Everyone can make a mistake, Len; even you.'

'Who says I'm making a mistake?'

'All right you're not. I've never known a man yet who would admit he's wrong. O.K. then it's not a mistake to be tied up in a job with a girl who's got a boy friend who's a private detective. That doesn't sound like a mistake does it? So you go ahead and walk into it. The trap's there, you walk into it. You let her get you into the dock and you'll stand there like the fool she's making of you and you'll get your seven years. Only don't imagine I'll be around when you come out. You'll be no use to me once you're inside, and seven years is a hell of a long time Len.'

Len Carron got up out of his chair and walked backwards and forwards across the room a couple of times. He stopped by a side table to mix himself a drink, a thing he didn't often do. He felt completely thrown by what Stella had told him and he didn't know how to deal with it.

Finally he came to a halt.

'Listen, Stella, I don't think this girl's a nark; I'm not going to think that, but all the same I wish to God I'd never started in on this ransom business, it's not my line.'

'Of course it isn't. Who talked you into it anyway? Whose idea was it?'

'Hers. She suggested it.'

'What a surprise. O.K. She's not a nark, then. Maybe she isn't. Just one of those tearaway Lefties, but if she's got a boy friend who's a private detective she's dangerous, Len.'

'I'll say she is.'

'Ditch her.'

'How?'

'Let her steal this picture she's so keen on. Why not? Only you keep right out of it. If she does steal it and gets picked up can the Law connect her with you?'

'Only if she talks; and even then it would only be what she said. No, they couldn't pin anything on me. If she gave them my name they would be round to question me of course—'

'Only you needn't be there need you?'

'I suppose not.'

'Of course you needn't. Tell her it's all set; let her go ahead and have her bit of Leftie fun. Let her fall out with the Law if she wants to. Whilst she's doing that you and I can be on the plane to Marbella and we could stay there for a month in the sun, couldn't we, Len? You leave it to me.'

THIRTEEN

'Who is it speaking, please?'

'C.I.D. HERE. Can I help you?'

'I'm talking about Mr Julius Bern's house, Pine Place—'

'Mr Julius Bern, Pine Place. Yes, right. Mrs Bern is it?'

'For God's sake, there isn't a Mrs Bern and you ought to know that. Pine Place, Acacia Road, St John's Wood.'

Detective Sergeant Fitt made a quick pencilled note on his pad and asked, 'And who is it speaking, please?'

'Never mind who it is speaking. I'm giving you some information. Are you listening?'

'Go ahead madam.'

'Mr Bern bought a picture a month or two back. At Christie's. It's called *Woman with a Flageolet.*'

'Woman with a what?'

'I'll spell it.' Stella did so and added, 'He paid a quarter of a million pounds for it.'

'At Christie's?'

'Check it if you want to.'

'I'm only just getting the facts down, madam. And what's happening to this picture now?'

'A girl has got Mr Bern's permission to copy it. She's spun him a yarn about being an art student. She *is* copying it, too; only that isn't all. She's going to steal the picture and screw ransom money out of Bern for returning it.'

Sergeant Robert Fitt did some quick thinking. In the course of a year a great deal of information came to the C.I.D. just as this particular piece was coming—anonymously, over the telephone. It was all investigated. Fitt knew from experience that about fifty per cent of 'information received' turned out to be fantasy stuff—nervous old ladies imagining things; or Walter Mittys who were anxious for any chance of getting their names linked with dramatic happenings; thirty per cent of the calls he got, Fitt reckoned, originated in personal spite, someone had taken a scunner against the next-door neighbours and intended to get at them any way they could; ten per cent were fakes pure and simple; probably the result of too many beers in the local or a bet, *wouldn't it be fun to ring up those bastards in blue and get them buzzing around in their cars all over the shop;* and that left the residue of ten per cent which were genuine and which sometimes led to something.

Listening on the telephone you couldn't be sure what sort you were dealing with so you had learned to be patient and polite (yes madam; thank you madam; that's very helpful madam;) you learnt not to scare your informant off with too many and too eager questions; you learnt to apply the basic rule of police work—get it down on paper, put a time and a date to it and, if possible, a name and address.

'This art student who's making a copy of the picture, can you tell us anything about her, madam?'

'Her name's Virginia Cave. She's done some acting. She's one of these Left-wing extremists. Militants. Out to smash everything up. She says so herself.'

'And you say she is planning to steal this picture from Mr Bern?'

'On Wednesday next. She'll just walk out with it. Wrapped up, of course. The staff have seen her coming in and out day after day with a canvas of some sort under her arm and they won't question her.'

'And Mr Bern?' but the line had gone dead; Sergeant Fitt's informant had evidently decided that she had said enough and had rung off.

Considerably later that day Fitt talked the matter over with his Inspector, Fred Corby.

The Sergeant had done a good deal of checking since the anonymous telephone call and was ready to answer the Inspector's questions.

'This woman who rang up—what sort was she?'

'Difficult to say. She had a reasonably well-educated voice. I wouldn't call it a posh voice; I wouldn't think she was a lady, but she'd got all her wits about her, I'd say. She wasn't a fool. Rang up from a call box.'

'And she's not in love with Miss Virginia Cave?'

'It didn't sound like it.'

'A bit of female spite do you think? Two women after one man?'

'Could be. Could well be. But that doesn't matter much if the information she gave us is true, does it?'

'Not in the slightest. Where should we poor ignoramuses in the C.I.D. be without the envy, malice and uncharitableness which, thank God, women bear so constantly in their loving hearts?'

Sergeant Fitt grinned. 'Where indeed?'

'Virginia Cave—what did you find out about her?'

'Pretty much what the informant said; she's done a bit of acting, nothing notable apparently and she's one of these well-heeled Left-wing intellectuals—demos and marches and all that stuff.'

'Well-heeled?'

'Her parents live in Eaton Square; but I haven't done much questioning yet. I don't want to frighten the bird away.'

'Quite right. Go easy at the moment.'

'What's the position up at the house, Pine Place?'

'I've had a chat with our local people; they know all about Julius Bern. Apparently he's loaded. He's got a collection of valuable pictures up there. And he did give two hundred and fifty thousand for a picture at Christie's nearly three months ago. I've checked that.'

'Two hundred and fifty thousand!' The Inspector did a bit of quick calculation. 'Do you realise that he's paying over seventeen thousand quid *a year* for the privilege of looking at the thing?'

Fitt laughed a little ruefully and said, 'Makes what we get for a full year's work look a bit silly, doesn't it?'

'What's the picture called again?'

'*Woman with a Flageolet* by a man called van Dysen.'

'I'll bet van Dysen didn't get a quarter of a million for painting it.'

'You're on a safe bet there, sir.'

'This man Bern, he'll have a security system to protect these pictures of his?'

'Oh yes. The pictures are all in what he calls his gallery; it hasn't got any windows and the door has an alarm that rings direct into our local station, and there are a couple of guards with Alsatian dogs who patrol the garden, one by day, one at night.'

'And how does Miss Cave propose to bring off her little coup? Strangle the Alsatian, do a bit of judo on a fourteen stone security man and leave old Bern himself tied up in a corner?'

Fitt laughed and said, 'By God, I wouldn't put all that past some of these militant intellectuals; they're a bloody sight more militant than they are intellectual. And when she's done all that she'll no doubt appeal to the Council of Civil Liberties to protect her from the brutal police. No, our local people up there told me a few things about Julius Bern which make me think the coup would be worked a bit differently from that.'

'Such as?'

'If we had Bern followed into the West End I reckon we should find him in Soho doing the round of the sex shops. The local rumour is that he has got quite a collection of porn tucked away in a little private room at Pine Place. As I read the scenario he's a d.o.m. who's delighted to get an attractive young woman—she's twenty-four apparently—into his house. She'll have played that side of things up for all it's worth; and she's on a good wicket; when you get an old man of seventy who thinks he has found a sexy young woman whose interested in his fly-buttons, she doesn't have to try to make a fool of him; he does it for her. Without his realising it she's got him where she wants him. Given that general set-up I don't think Miss Cave is going to find it too difficult to get rid of Bern in some way or other for half an hour and walk out with the wrapped-up picture under her arm; like our informant said as far as the security men are concerned she's an art student who has been o-kayed by the boss; they're used to her going in and out every day carrying a picture of some sort.'

'And all this is due to happen next Wednesday?'

'That's the whisper.'

'Have you said anything to Bern yet?'

'Not a word. And I don't intend to. People in Bern's frame of mind don't recognise the truth even if you spell it out for them with coloured illustrations. If we warn the old fool he'll be quite capable of thinking that we are persecuting an innocent girl and he would very likely pass the warning on to her. No, a word to Bern will mean that the thing will be called off and we shall be left empty-handed.'

The Inspector nodded his agreement; he had long since been of the opinion that the less you told the damn-fool public about what you were doing in their interest the better. 'There'll be a getaway car waiting in Acacia Road presumably,' he said.

'Sure to be.'

'So what's your plan of action.'

'It won't be difficult to spot the car; it will be waiting close to the house with a villain in it. Very likely two of them. We'll have somebody handy to deal with that and we'll pick up the girl just as she comes out into the road with the stolen picture under her arm.'

'And so we'll save a rich man quite a bit of ransom money?'

'Frankly, sir, I'm not interested in that. These old men in mackintoshes who trudge round the porn shops whether they're millionaires or misers get my goat. I haven't any time for them. Straightforward sex—O.K.; all this song and dance to remind yourself of what you believe you were once capable of isn't so good. But I don't like thieving villains and if we can catch one so much the better.'

VIRGINIA WAS feeling on top of the world these days. Things were going her way. The plan to steal the van Dysen had been hers and hers alone and it was working out unbelievably well. Unbelievably that is until you took human nature into account. Thinking over how easily she had pulled the wool over Bern's eyes Virginia was sometimes amused, sometimes disgusted. She found the pawing, panting, brushing-up-against-you-by-accident-isn't-that-a-lovely-feeling business revolting. She submitted to it, even managed, as she hoped to give an impression of enjoying it by reminding herself that she was an actress. Not that any work came her way these days; her agent didn't ring up and she didn't bother to go and see him; she had written a one-act play for herself in which she was author, producer, and sole star.

More than once Len had asked her, 'Do you think Bern suspects anything?'

'Not a thing. Not a damned thing. Once he starts looking at those porny photos of his he can't think of anything else. His mind goes. If I walked into Pine Place carrying a Tommy gun and a hatchet he'd think it was some sort of kinky game and start getting steamed up about it.'

'Men are pretty bloody silly when it comes to sex, you reckon?'

Virginia answered him by laughing. She hoped that he understood the laugh. The laugh meant how right you are, Len; and just at the minute you yourself are being pretty bloody silly over that smart little red-headed bitch of yours—*of yours?* She isn't 'of yours'; she wasn't sitting in the getaway car for the wages snatch that went wrong was she? She didn't come up with this marvellous idea of just walking off with a picture worth a quarter of a million, did she?

Virginia didn't say anything of this; she just laughed; she had learnt that you had to go very carefully with Len; she had been able to boss Roddy

Marten, she could kick him around; any attempt to kick Len around was apt to be dangerous and counter-productive. And in the last day or two, ever since agreeing Wednesday as D-day, she had noticed a subtle difference in Len. It was difficult to describe it exactly, just as it was difficult to guess what it was due to, or might mean.

But it was there.

Sometimes she thought it might be suppressed excitement because the coup was finally to be brought off; sometimes she flattered herself that it was satisfaction with her for having thought the whole thing up and made it possible.

Which of these explanations was valid, and indeed whether either of them was, she didn't know; but she was aware of *something.* A person can speak, look and act normally and yet your antennae can be picking up some thing extra all the time of which you are aware but which you cannot put a name to.

Although she was aware of these 'atmospherics' Virginia felt that she could afford not to worry overmuch about them at the moment. She herself was caught up in the excitement of bringing off her scheme triumphantly. That what she planned to do was theft didn't worry her in the slightest. Early on when she had first proposed the idea to him Len had teased her with 'You've become a real villain, Ginny. You're going round stealing now.'

'All property is theft, all ownership is.'

'Oh my God, don't start your political stuff. All ownership theft? What bloody nonsense. Old Bern paid two hundred and fifty thousand quid for the picture we're talking about. A quarter of a million! Don't you reckon that entitles him to it? It's his; he owns it; he paid for it. You go into a shop in Oxford Street and buy a hat, isn't it yours?'

'I never wear a hat.'

'For Chrissake, how is it possible to argue with a woman!'

Nor did she worry about what was going to happen once she had got the van Dysen away (as she was quite certain she could) from Pine Place. St Albans? Chalky? She didn't bother to ask questions about them anymore. Len was fixing all that; that was his side of the coup. And she didn't doubt that he would fix it properly. All she would have to do was to go where she was told and do as she was told. Obey orders. She didn't object to that, as long as Len was giving the orders. And ultimately when Len had got his hands on the cash she didn't think it would be too difficult to make him get rid of the red-head—after all the red-head wouldn't have had anything to do with getting him the cash he loved so much, would she?...

Meanwhile there was the sheer fun of the game itself.

'And how is Mrs Goddard's back today?'

'Much the same as usual, Miss; thank you for asking. I always tell the wife when you ask after her and she takes it very kindly.'

'I'm always sorry for people with any sort of physical trouble. I've got a limp myself, I expect you've noticed it?'

'Well, I did notice something Miss, but naturally I didn't like to say anything. An accident was it?'

'I was born with it.'

'Oh dear; well we can't help what we are born with can we?'

'It doesn't worry me now, except that humping those frames and canvases around sometimes gets tiring.'

'I'm sure it does. I've noticed you're always carrying something. That's being an artist I suppose?'

'A queer lot artists,' Virginia assured him.

The security man laughed. 'It takes all sorts,' he said sagely.

Nor did Lessing pose any problems. Albert Lessing understood his master perfectly, and very largely sympathised with him. Julius Bern might have his funny little ways but in Lessing's opinion his income entitled him to them. So it was, 'Good morning, Miss. Nice to see you again. You'll be up in the gallery painting again today will you?'

'It's getting towards the end now.'

'Mr Bern's waiting for you in the study if you care to come this way, Miss.'

Lessing had no doubts about what Julius Bern was getting out of the arrangement; as to what the girl got out of it he was not so sure. A nice fat cheque, possibly, or some jewellery; and at any rate as far as the painting business went she seemed genuinely to enjoy that. However good the reports which Lessing brought back to the servants' quarters Mrs Lessing remained unconvinced.

'I'm surprised at you Albert. But then again I'm not, not really. All men are the same. Always on about the one thing. The way you men go on you'd think there was nothing in the world to think about except naked women. I think a gentleman like Mr Bern ought to know better; and as for the girl—well!'

'I've tried to explain to you before Ada, Miss Cave is an artist.'

'Artist?' Ada Lessing snorted. 'And she sets up to be a bit of an actress, too, doesn't she?'

'I wouldn't know about that.'

'Well, I know about it. I read a piece in the *Express* yesterday about this Equity thing where it said Miss Virginia Cave was one of the militant lot. That girl's a militant, Albert.'

'She's not doing anything militant here, is she? Sitting down quietly making a copy of a picture.'

'As long as she doesn't try to run the house.'

'Run the house? What on earth are you getting at now?'

'Old men can make fools of themselves where women are concerned. A girl like that can twist an old man round her little finger.'

'I don't think anything like that is going on.'

'Why did she ask you about cleaning the silver on a Wednesday afternoon, then? What's it got to do with her?'

'It was just a question. She's interested in what goes on.'

'I'll bet she is.'

'IT'S NICE to see you again, Mr Hefferman,' said Mrs Drew.

As was his custom when visiting Hove, Hooky was taking the precaution of fortifying himself against the rigours of dining with his Aunt.

'I was going to ask how you are Mrs D,' he said, 'but it's quite unnecessary. You look magnificent.'

Even Mrs Drew flushed slightly with pleasure at the compliment.

'Now Mr Hefferman,' she replied, 'it's very nice of you to say such things and I'm sure you've had lots of fun in your time, but you mustn't try it on with me, you know.'

'Mrs D,' Hooky answered, and he meant every word of what he said, 'I wouldn't presume to try anything on with you, I wouldn't dare.'

He enquired after the Professor and Mrs Drew said that she didn't think they would be seeing Doctor Stuart-Crawley for some time, 'Perhaps you haven't seen the *Argus* lately?' she asked.

Hooky had to admit that living as he did in London he had to be satisfied with a choice of what are arguably the two worst evening papers in the world.

'It was all in the *Argus,*' Mrs Drew said.

'About the Prof?'

'Some of the boys' parents complained and then, of course, there was trouble.'

'Oh dear, I hope nothing dreadful has happened to him?'

'Well, he had to resign. You couldn't expect anything else, even in these days, could you?'

'I suppose not.'

'He must have been upset by all the publicity—you know how the Press love anything of that kind—so I think he's just lying very low and not coming out at all. And do you know, Mr Hefferman, I miss him. Yes, it's quite true, I do. I genuinely miss him. Doctor Stuart-Crawley is a gentleman, and the way he talked, all that Latin and so on well, I'm not saying that I always understood it all, but it was an education to listen to him. Silly, isn't it?'

'What's silly, Mrs D?'

'Well, I mean, a man like that—he knows such a lot and there's so much he could do in life, and then to spoil it all by getting mixed up in this business with little boys—oh dear, having so much and then to throw it all away.'

'And who with Eden didst devise the Snake.'

Mrs Drew seemed quite startled. 'Say that again Mr Hefferman,' she requested.

Hooky said it again. 'There was Eden once,' he amplified 'Or was there? I don't know. I'm not sure. Eden. Cool and green and lovely and a man and a woman walking in it, happy. Then just for the hell of things whoever wrote the original scenario thought up the idea of the snake and slipped it into the long grass; *that'll stir things up* he must have said and, by Jiminy, it has.'

Mrs Drew was much impressed. 'When you talk like that,' she said, 'it's as good as listening to the Professor.'

Hooky held out his glass for replenishment. 'Before going over the top,' he said, 'every soldier is entitled to a heartening issue of rum. I'll settle for a Pimms, please, Mrs D.'

'Going over the top?'

'I should have said dining with my Aunt.'

'Go on with you, Mr Hefferman; there isn't a woman in the world you couldn't get your way with if you tried.'

Hooky wanted to say 'Is that a promise, Mrs D?' but he didn't dare.

Mrs Page-Foley was in an amiable mood. 'It does an old woman good to see you, Hooky,' she declared; 'I am even prepared to overlook your glaring faults for the breath of air you bring to this bridge-bound backwater. Do you know what a silly little bird-brained woman said to me the other day? "I suppose you're not interested in gardens," she said. Interested? Good heavens, when Digby and I lived at Mannocks we never had fewer than five gardeners and people used to come miles to see the rhododendrons and the all white border—*interested* indeed!'

'You reigned in some state.'

'Too much state, really. Some of it was nice. Some of it was silly.'

'Unfortunately so many nice things turn out to be silly.'

'I'm quite sure you know all about that. Have you been able to help Leo and Lois Chanderley at all?'

'In a negative way I think I possibly have.'

'You sound exactly like one of these waffling politicians on the TV picture machine. Have you managed to get in touch with this girl of theirs they are so worried about?'

'Several times.'

'And what is she up to?'

'Nothing as far as I can see. That is to say nothing unduly alarming. She just doesn't want to live at home. I expect she has a bit of a wild whirl around every now and again, but who doesn't?'

'I'm quite sure you do.'

Hooky desperately wanted to ask 'And didn't you when you were her age?' but of course, to do so was unthinkable. To his astonishment it turned out to be not only unthinkable but unnecessary.

'And so did I when I was her age,' Mrs Page-Foley said, a sudden smile softening her face and her old eyes glazed with memories of years long gone, 'but the things that Leo seemed worried about—drugs and demonstrations and all that kind of nonsense, is the girl going in for that?'

'Not as far as I can see. She's spending most of her time at the moment making a copy of a picture belonging to a rich old codger in St John's Wood.'

'Making a copy of a picture?'

'Virginia was trained as an art student apparently and she's still genuinely keen about it.'

'What sort of a picture?'

'I haven't seen it, but Julius Bern paid a quarter of a million pounds for it at Christie's earlier in the year.'

'A quarter of a million! No picture in the world is worth that.'

'Probably not,' Hooky agreed, 'but that's what Bern paid for it nevertheless. Maybe he was had for a sucker. I wouldn't think that happens often, though.'

'Who is this Julius Bern?'

'A Hebraic gentleman who gets rescued out of difficult deckchair situations and who has a lot of money.'

'I don't remember anyone of that name coming to Mannocks.'

'He probably wasn't on your visiting list, Aunt.'

'How old is he?'

'Well over seventy I'd guess.'

'The girl isn't likely to get into any trouble there, then.'

'That's precisely what I think,' Hooky said.

'And you still continue to see something of her?'

'We've got a date tomorrow evening.'

'You are taking the girl out to dinner somewhere?'

'Well, not exactly dinner, we're meeting at a place called The Good Soldier.'

'A public house! Really, Hooky! In my young days a lady didn't expect an evening out in the West End to consist of a visit to a public house!'

'In your young days, Aunt, dinner for two in the West End didn't cost twenty-five pounds.'

'Twenty-five pounds! I should say not; we had more sense.'

'There's still plenty of sense about, but not so much money; so we have to do the best we can.'

'Are you by any chance getting interested in this girl Hooky?' Mrs Page-Foley asked sharply.

The truth was that Hooky *was* finding himself more and more interested in Virginia these days. Whatever Mr Pope might say on the subject Hooky Hefferman was convinced, and had been for a long time, that the proper study of mankind was woman; experience had taught him that all women were delightfully different, all women were dangerously and devastatingly the same. There were contradictions in Virginia he found intriguing and—if he was honest with himself—he had to admit that he found it slightly galling not to be able to make more headway with her. She was willing enough to meet him in The Good Soldier occasionally but even there her moods were unpredictable. There were times—when she was talking about her soldier brother for instance—when he felt close to reality with her; there were other times, wild, Left-wing irresponsible chatter-box times, when he felt that she ought to be upended across his knee and spanked hard; but there was one thing always true of Virginia, she didn't bother to talk about anything unless it meant something to her, what she was talking about at the moment she believed in.

The day after visiting his Aunt in Hove, Hooky was due to meet Virginia in The Good Soldier at half-past seven. Normally he was a punctual person, not subscribing to the modern view that as long as you suited your own convenience it didn't matter how long you kept everybody else waiting, but this particular day turned out to be one of those occasions when the spiteful gods take charge.

First of all there was confusion at the squash courts over the booking and so some delay in starting the game; then right at the very end Hooky's opponent snapped an Achilles tendon and arrangements had to be made to get a cab, ring up his wife and see that he was safely on his way home. By the time Hooky had had his shower and changed he was inevitably late. A full twenty minutes late he realised, glancing at his watch as he pushed open the door of the Saloon Bar.

Being by now fairly well used to Virginia's propensity for flying off the handle at short notice if she imagined herself slighted in any way he would not have been surprised to find her gone. But all was well. She was seated on one of the high stools at the bar talking to a man; a stranger at a loose end, Hooky imagined, optimistically on the look-out for local talent. Hooky, who had so often been in the same situation himself, felt a certain sympathy for the man; he didn't think the optimist would get very far with the PBP one.

He stood for a moment by the door watching the little scene with the amused interest which generally comes from seeing without being seen. To his surprise things suddenly took an unexpected turn. Virginia reached for her handbag which was lying on the counter, drew out a note and handed it to the man.

From his distant viewpoint Hooky could not be sure but it looked to him remarkably like a five pound note. Virginia distributing fivers? Being an inquisitive sort of cuss by nature Hooky was interested. Whether a oner or a fiver the note seemed to satisfy the stranger. It was clearly his congee. Stuffing the paper money in his pocket he turned and left, brushing by Hooky in the doorway without looking at him.

'So you've decided to come at last,' was Virginia's greeting—decidedly prickly this evening Hooky realised, and who could blame her?

'I'm sorry,' he said amicably, 'I apologise; but disasters befell.'

'I imagine you're the sort of person who attracts disasters. I was just about to go. I don't like being kept waiting around for anybody.'

'Will Sir have his usual and Madam a replenishment?' Cyril asked from behind the bar; and in order to give any flames of dissension that there might be an encouraging little puff he added, 'Madam has been expecting Sir for some time.'

Hooky smiled at him. A deceptive smile; he was thinking *one day I'll get into my cups and do that smooth-hipped little troublemaker a mischief; I'll crown him with one of his own pint pots.* Aloud he said, 'But Madam found company to entertain her.'

'An actor,' Virginia volunteered. 'Hard up, of course because he's out of work. Do you realise that at any time, at this moment, now, more than fifty per cent of the people in the theatrical profession are out of work?'

Serves the silly twits right for having gone into the theatrical profession Hooky felt like saying, why couldn't they have opted to do something useful? been bus conductors, train drivers, postmen. He had the sense not to say anything of the sort. What he did say, to Cyril, was, 'A little more borage, Cyril, please.'

Virginia had no intention of being put off by the diversionary tactic. She was annoyed at having been kept waiting and by other matters and she proposed to vent her annoyance on someone.

'You don't seem to mind that half the acting profession is permanently out of work?' she said aggressively.

'If I really thought about it I expect I'd burst into tears,' Hooky told her, 'but we've all got problems.'

'In a properly run state the arts would be looked after by the whole community. In the Communist countries artists of all kinds are treated as heroes.'

'Unless they happen to say the wrong thing, of course, then they get the chop. Talking about artists how are you getting on up at Pine Place?'

'Everything is going splendidly. Everything.'

Hooky was slightly surprised at the note of suppressed excitement which was suddenly detectable in the girl's voice.

'You're really enjoying copying the van Dysen aren't you?' he asked.

'It's a most marvellous painting. You simply don't realise how wonderful it is until you look into it, examine it minutely, literally square inch by square inch.'

'You ought to have been an artist instead of going on the stage.'

'I suppose that means you don't think I'm any good as an actress?'

'Now did I say that? Cyril, did I say anything of the sort?'

Cyril said he was sure Sir wouldn't say anything rude about Madam; not that he had actually been listening, he was just naturally interested in anything that Sir or Madam said.

'All right, all right. Sorry if I sounded a bit sharp. Not that I'm really sorry. I *am* sharp. What's the use of being any other way? Nothing's any good unless it's got an edge to it. And I don't believe I'm such a bad actress as all that anyway. It wasn't my fault that the thing at the Haymarket folded.'

'Of course it wasn't. You were good in it.'

'I wonder if you mean that—I sometimes wonder if you mean anything you say.'

'Not much of it.'

'My God, men! But you're not as clever as all that, you know. You can easily be made fools of.'

'Only too easily. Whom are you making a fool of at the moment?'

'Wouldn't you like to know? And anyway who says I'm making a fool of anybody? I'm spending all my time copying—*trying* to copy—a most wonderful picture.'

'*All* your time? What about Julius Bern? What's he getting out of it?'

'Julius Bern is a damned nuisance, all this fingering and fumbling—*ugh.*'

'Have a heart. Bern's an old man. Desire doth outrun performance; his performance may be suspect, but you can't blame the old boy for still having the desire.'

'I blame all men for everything.'

Hooky caught Cyril's eye. Cyril was busy polishing a glass. He said nothing but every flick of his deftly used polishing cloth spoke for him—*if you will get mixed up with these fierce female creatures what do you expect?*

'Has Bern got a lot of pictures up there?' Hooky asked.

'There's a whole gallery; not that it's very large but it's packed with canvases, all Dutch and all lovely.'

'Anything else?'

Virginia paused for a moment and then asked, 'What else should there be?'

'Nothing I suppose. A gallery stuffed with Dutch masterpieces is enough to go on with. Things being as they are presumably somebody will break in and scoff the lot one day—or has friend Bern invested in some pretty useful safety precautions? What's the security like?'

'What do you want to know about the security arrangements for?'

There was a note in the girl's voice which Hooky was conscious of, but which he misread; she can't seriously think that I'm planning a raid on the place he told himself; but in case she might be thinking along those lines and just for fun he said aloud, 'I'm planning to raid Pine Place one of these days. A picture that fetches a quarter of a million at Christie's must be worth stealing.'

Virginia laughed. 'You'll find that you're wasting your time,' she assured him.

Hooky spent about half an hour in The Good Soldier before the final explosion came. It was a curious thirty minutes, and Hooky, usually in his element and in command of things in a pub, never felt on this particular evening at his ease.

Considering the matter he was inclined to put it down to a bad start; he had got off on the wrong foot by being twenty minutes late and Virginia wasn't going to let him forget it. Not for the first time she was proving a good deal more prickly than possible. The prickliness Hooky was used to; but this evening there was something else which, because he couldn't understand it, he found faintly worrying; Virginia had an air of suppressed excitement about her almost, as she might have had, Hooky thought, if she were waiting for the curtain to go up; what's biting the girl he wondered more than once...

'And anyway *why* were you late?' she suddenly demanded, returning to her pet grievance of the evening like a dog going back to a favourite bone.

'An Achilles tendon. My chum's Achilles tendon went twang; like a violin string snapping; and being the chivalrous, kind-hearted Good Samaritan that you know me to be I had to rally round and render help.'

'Achilles tendon!' Virginia laughed derisively. 'My God, what marvellous excuses men think up. Not that it mattered; I was perfectly happy here on my own.'

'Except of course that you weren't on your own. You had your out-of-work actor pal to talk to.'

'I suppose you have no sympathy for anybody like that; you're a typical product of a capitalistic society.'

'Absolutely typical,' Hooky agreed amiably, 'decadent, debilitated, dehydrated, and dehydration is a very serious matter—another Pimms, Cyril, if you please.'

'You drink far too much,' Virginia said. 'It's so stupid. All men do it, I suppose they think they have to in order to prove they are men.'

'There are other ways of proving it,' Hooky pointed out mildly. 'Does Len drink too much, too?'

'You can leave Len out of it. I don't propose to discuss him with you. But actually, since you ask, no, Len doesn't drink too much. He's got more sense.'

'Bully for Len,' Hooky said, watching the preparation of his Pimms with approving interest. 'What's his line of business, by the way, what does he do for a living?'

'Is that anything to do with you?'

'Nothing whatsoever. I asked out of mere curiosity.'

'Ask no questions and you'll be told no lies.'

'That's what I'm afraid of,' Hooky said. 'No lies? Where should we be without lies? Lies are the greater part of civilised life. Where would religion, politics and the business of marriage be without serious, sustained and systematic lying?'

'Sir is cynical,' Cyril said pushing the now completed Pimms forward.

'And I hate cynics,' Virginia declared. 'I like people who believe in things, do things.'

'You like men of action?'

'Of course I do. I like action, action's fun, exciting.'

'You ought to marry a soldier. Some nice chubby-faced spit and polish Sandhurst type complete with shining sword and snorting steed.'

'My God, you are smug aren't you? What makes you think you are so superior to anyone who happened to go to Sandhurst?'

By now Hooky realised the gaffe he had made and was dismayed; he was hardly surprised at the way Virginia had suddenly blazed out.

'Look,' he stammered trying to mend a situation which was already clearly past mending, 'I'm most frightfully sorry—'

'What for?' Virginia demanded icily. 'For being impertinent enough to tell me I ought to marry a soldier? There'll soon be plenty of action without me marrying anybody, don't worry about that. To hell with you anyway.'

She left an unfinished drink on the bar, strode across the saloon and disappeared into the street leaving behind an uncomfortable silence for some seconds. Eventually Cyril broke it by saying, 'Madam appears to be rather touchy about some things.'

'You can say that again,' Hooky agreed, but privately he was upset at his own performance, it was just crass stupidity not to have remembered about the soldier brother and Northern Ireland, and he didn't like to be guilty of crass stupidity especially where a woman was concerned. He sipped reflectively at his Pimms.

'Sir is thinking,' Cyril said.

Hooky nodded; he certainly was thinking. He was thinking that there had been something odd about the whole interlude with Virginia; she was clearly peeved at his being late; that was straightforward and understandable; what he didn't understand was the undertone of excitement which he was sure he had detected in the girl as though she were waiting for something to happen...*there'll soon be plenty of action.* What the devil had she meant by that, now?

'The bright moth of curiosity flutters dangerously round the tempting flame of incomprehension,' he pointed out to Cyril, 'Chu Ling. A Chinese gentleman, perhaps you know him?'

'I've known a lot of gentlemen,' Cyril said, 'but I've never taken a fancy to anything Oriental.'

Hooky drained his tall glass and set it down; with a nod to Cyril he turned to go. He thought, erroneously, that the evening was over.

In Grafton Street, not six yards from the doorway of The Good Soldier, he found himself confronting the out-of-work actor, the recipient of five pound notes. Hooky had no idea what had brought the man back there but he had no intention of letting him go unquestioned.

'Your girl friend has gone,' he told him. 'She left about ten minutes ago.'

'That's good news,' Roddy Marten said. 'That being the case I think I'll go inside; after all, why pass a good pub?'

'Why indeed?' Hooky agreed; it was clear that the stranger had already converted a fair proportion of his fiver into liquid assets and Hooky realised that he must tread warily; drunks, he well knew, had to be handled carefully.

By the time they reached the bar Marten had done a certain amount of thinking himself. 'And who the hell are you anyway?' he asked. 'A pal of Virginia's I suppose?'

'An admirer of her acting,' Hooky told him.

'I don't think much of your judgment, then. I could act her off the stage any day. Any day at all; if I got the chance. And what do you know about acting anyway?'

'Not much. Nothing really.'

'Are you a critic or something? Christ, you look just like a critic come to think of it. Are you in the chair or am I?'

'Just tell Cyril what you want, it's my pleasure. Cyril—'

Cyril was all attention. 'It's a pleasure to see Sir again so soon,' he declared.

The double Scotch which Marten ordered did something to mollify him in the direction of amiability.

'Well, if you're so effing ignorant about acting,' he said, 'what else don't you know anything about?'

'Life, I suppose. Pretty well everything.'

'You'll run on the rocks then, won't you? You'll end up a bloody shipwreck.'

'That's only too likely I'm afraid.'

'I'll tell you something, then. I'll give you a piece of good advice—not that people take advice; people are too bloody stupid to take advice. You look to me like the sort of person who wouldn't take advice from anyone. Right?'

By God if you carry on like this you'll be getting more than advice, Hooky thought, *you'll be getting the bloodiest of bloody noses;* he was beginning to regret having teamed up with this boring lush, yet instinct still raised a faint hope that he might get something out of him, so aloud he said peacefully, 'I'm always in the market for any wisdom that's going. A snapper up of unconsidered trifles.'

'Are you trying to be clever, soldier? What trifles? Who said anything about trifles?'

'W. Shakespeare actually.'

'Shakespeare? How the hell does he come into this? You're not paying attention. You want to be more careful. I was talking to a girl in this pub, at this very bar, earlier this evening. You want to be very careful with her, I can tell you.'

'Why is that?' Hooky asked quietly.

'You know this girl? The one I was talking to? Virginia Cave, the celebrated actress. Celebrated my arse. You know her do you?'

'How on earth should I know her?' Hooky said.

'No. Well. If ever you do come across her you ask her how Len is. That'll shake her.'

'Len?'

'This bird left me to go to Len—can you believe that?'

Only too easily Hooky thought, but he didn't say it; what he said, speaking gently and persuasively, was, 'And who is Len exactly?'

'I'll tell you who Len is, and I don't mind who hears me say it. Len Carron is a villain, a crook. He dreams up schemes for stealing things; makes a balls of it; and then blames somebody else because it went wrong. I expect the two of them are cooking up a scheme to steal something at this very moment. And as for Virginia being an actress—do you know that I did *two years* with the Winchester Rep? Two years in rep. That's where you learn the business. Comedy, tragedy, farce, classics, kitchen sink stuff—the lot. Why if I were to tell you the parts I've played—'

'Another time,' said Hooky, who had suffered before from the interminable loquacity of narcissistic actors 'I'm afraid I must be going.'

'You're not interested in hearing about my stage career?'

'Some other time. Goodnight.'

'Perhaps Sir will be back again in a minute or two?' Cyril said archly.

'Not tonight, Josephine,' Hooky reassured him.

FOURTEEN

More pieces in a jigsaw

DETECTIVE INSPECTOR Fred Corby was not in a good temper. At home the boiler had not come on automatically as it should have done at six-thirty and consequently he had had to go without his morning bath. His wife had not been particularly sympathetic. She pointed out that on three separate occasions lately she had reminded him that the heating engineers should be asked to come and look at the boiler which was giving warning signs of trouble and on three separate occasions Fred had undertaken to do this and then completely forgotten.

So bathless, and smarting under the irritating reflection that in some mysterious way women who really knew nothing about anything generally turned out to be right about everything, the Inspector confronted his Sergeant.

'I've no time for these so-called private eyes,' he said testily. 'I suppose they're O.K. for some things—what happened to Auntie Meg who lost her memory and went missing four years ago and did the co-respondent stay all night and come out in the morning doing up his flies; that sort of stuff; but real police work, never. They're just a pain in the neck, they get in the way.'

Sergeant Fitt stood his ground; the Inspector was clearly a bit tetchy this morning; had a bit of a barney with his missus probably; not a difficult thing to do, Fitt thought, from what he knew of Mrs Corby; and in any case, he reflected, they all tend to get like this; the higher up you go the more you lose touch with reality. Sergeant Fitt had once attended a meeting of police officers especially paraded to listen to an address by the Home Secretary. He and one hundred and fifty other hard-working officers had listened in bewilderment which only a strong sense of discipline prevented from degenerating into derisive hilarity; as a fellow sergeant had said to him on the way out 'These boys at the top must live in a different world from us. Cloud cuckoo land. They haven't the vaguest idea what's really going on. It's either very funny or desperately serious, and I'm damned if I know which.'

Inspector Fred Corby had much more sense of reality than the Home Secretary of course, but even he had a bit of a blind spot on this private eye question.

'I've had some useful info off this chap at times,' Fitt maintained. 'He knows a lot of villains.'

'Probably a villain himself.'

'Who isn't?'

'Well, if you've got time to waste, you may as well waste it having a word with him. Go ahead. He won't have anything useful to tell you; but if he has, let me know.'

That's what they call keeping their options open, Fitt thought as he made his way back to his own small office.

'Well then,' Hooky greeted the Sergeant, 'how are you? And how's the Inspector? How's your superior officer?'

Sergeant Fitt grinned slightly. 'A bit sharp this morning,' he had to admit. 'Probably got out of bed on the wrong side. He doesn't like you lot much.'

'There's gratitude for you,' said Hooky, 'think of all the pints of beer I've stood you in times past.'

'That wouldn't impress the Inspector much, he's a teetotaller.'

'No wonder the Force is degenerating—a teetotal Detective Inspector—it's a contradiction in terms.'

Fitt laughed. 'What's on the menu today?' he asked. 'What unlikely bit of information are you bringing in?'

'None. I want something off you. I want to hear anything you know about a character called Len Carron.'

If the query had stumped him Fitt could have had recourse to the vast mine of information held by the

C.R.O.; but as it happened he didn't have to; like every good C.I.D. officer he carried a remarkably comprehensive Rogues Gallery in his own head and he knew enough about Len Carron to answer.

'Len Carron? If I've got him right, and I think I have, he's a hold-up merchant. Wage snatching. Money coming back from the bank. Not one of the big boys. Nothing sensational. Useful little touches of ten or twelve thousand, that sort of thing. But we haven't had any trouble from Lennie for a couple of years now.'

'Does he ever steal anything other than cash?'

'As far as I remember he prefers cash if he can get it, but Lennie's a villain, given the chance he'd steal anything. What makes you interested in Len Carron?'

'I've discovered that a client of mine is a friend of his.'

'You do mix in bad company, don't you? Who's your client, somebody else known to us?'

'She's a Miss Virginia Cave.'

Sergeant Fitt would certainly have won a medal at RADA for the complete impassiveness with which he greeted this altogether unexpected piece of news.

'Miss Cave is a client of yours?' he asked.

'Well, no, actually she isn't. I'm acting for her family, her father and mother. The girl has been mixed up in a number of these demos and sit-ins and similar idiocies and naturally they are worried about her.'

'And you say she knows Len Carron?'

'Yes, she certainly knows him. Maybe she's his girl friend of the moment, leaping in and out of his bed. I don't know.'

'No doubt she's got the artistic temperament,' the Sergeant said.

'After what you've just told me about Len Carron I'm as worried as her parents are. That silly girl has got herself into bad company.'

'She certainly has if she has teamed up with Carron,' Fitt assured him.

Half an hour later the Sergeant was reporting the interview to his Inspector. In the interim Mrs Corby had rung up to say that the maintenance men had been to look at the boiler and that everything was now in working order again, Fred Corby was therefore in a considerably better mood and he greeted Fitt almost jocularly.

'So what invaluable piece of information did your precious private eye turn up with?' he demanded.

'Actually he came to see if I could help him with a bit of inside knowledge.'

'I'll bet he did. These boys aren't exactly backward in coming forward when they want something. What was he after?'

'He was asking about a villain called Len Carron.'

'Len Carron?' The Inspector carried in his memory a similar sort of Rogues Gallery to the one possessed by his junior officer, but it was less sharp and less accurate. 'I seem to remember the name,' Corby said, 'but I can't quite—'

'He's on the books right enough. Wage snatches. A couple of small jobs. So far he seems to have steered clear of anything big.'

'Wise man. S.P.Q.R. Small profits quick returns.'

'This private eye—Hefferman his name is—told me a very interesting thing about Len Carron.'

'Such as?'

'He told me the name of Carron's current girl friend.'

'And you found that interesting?'

'So will you. It's Miss Virginia Cave.'

This totally unexpected piece of news delighted the Inspector. It was one more example of something he had experienced time and time again during his years in the force, that often enough cases got solved and villains caught as much by pieces of gratuitous luck as by anything else. The important thing was not to turn Lady Luck away when she smiled on you.

'Well, well, well,' he said, 'that *is* interesting. Is Carron going in for the picture stealing and ransom demanding business then?'

'It looks very much like it. I can't see this girl Cave trying to work the racket on her own; she's much more likely to have been put up to it by a professional villain.'

'Carron ought to have more sense. He ought to stick to his own line. I suppose he'll be in the get-away car tomorrow then?'

'Sure to be. When you come to think of it, it's rather a neat job, really. The girl has properly pulled the wool over randy old Julius Bern's eyes; she'll just walk out, unchallenged, with the picture under her arm and friend Lennie will be waiting in a stolen car in Acacia Road—only of course our lot will be there too.'

'Highly satisfactory,' the Inspector said. 'You didn't give this man Hefferman any hint that we already knew something about Virginia Cave did you?'

'Not on your life,' the Sergeant, quite inaccurately, assured him.

HOOKY FOUND his interview with Sergeant Fitt disturbing. He had known for some time that 'Len' was a figure in Virginia's background, and now Len turned out to be a genuine dyed-in-the-wool crook. It was easy enough to come to the decision that Len, together with Virginia's relations with him, would have to be much more thoroughly investigated, but it wasn't until later that evening, when he was undressing, moving about his bedroom, going through the ritual—emptying of trouser pockets—small change in one place, keys in another—that suddenly out of the blue, something Detective Sergeant Fitt had said occurred to him with startling force.

...no doubt she's got the artistic temperament the Sergeant had said...

Artistic temperament? What the devil did the C.I.D. people know about Virginia being an artist? Was it possible that she was really up to some mischief at Pine Place and that they were on to her already? Hooky's conscience, which often had long periods off duty, smote him; he realised that he had not been taking his guardian angel role seriously enough. Tomorrow, he determined, he would make amends...

THERE WAS no answer to the top flat bell and Hooky stood for a moment or two in the hall, undecided. The door of the ground floor flat opened and a man and a woman came out carrying suitcases. Hooky had a notion that he had seen the woman before, but now she was dressed for travelling and the light in the entrance hall was indifferent and he could not be sure. She, however, was quite sure that she had seen him before, and her heartbeat quickened a little.

'I was hoping to find Miss Cave in,' Hooky said. 'You don't happen to know when she'll be back do you?'

'Not the faintest idea,' the man answered. 'Why should I have?'

'I just wondered,' Hooky said mildly.

'Sorry. Can't help you.'

When they reached the car and were settled in their seats Stella said quietly, 'You know who that was I suppose?'

'Not the foggiest.'

'That's Virginia's boy friend, the private eye, so the sooner we get to Gatwick and on that plane the better.'

Len Carron, always a man for action rather than words, turned the ignition key and the engine came to life.

The belief—half belief—that he had seen the woman before somewhere nagged at Hooky's mind. He was disturbed by it, he had an uncomfortable feeling that he was missing something and he had no idea what it was.

When in doubt ask questions was a golden rule in Hooky's conduct of life; admittedly it was a rule which had landed him now and then in a good deal of trouble but nevertheless it was one which he still pursued enthusiastically. When he reached Acacia Road, however, he found himself answering questions rather than asking them. Goddard, Zena at his heels, was doing the asking.

'You want to see Mr Bern?' he queried.

'I do indeed. Rather urgently.'

Goddard chuckled. 'Ar, they all say it's urgent,' he said. 'Are you expected?'

Hooky, who never saw any point in telling the truth when a lie would serve better, instantly answered with great conviction 'Yes.'

'It's funny I haven't been told, then, isn't it?' Goddard asked.

'Hilarious. Perhaps you aren't told everything.'

'Look, mister, I'm the security man around here. I've got my instructions. You may be all right, you may have a bomb in your pocket. If I don't like the look of anyone they don't get to that front door. Zena and I see to that.'

I bet you'd be an awkward bastard in a scrap Hooky thought *and that damned dog looks a killer;* aloud, smiling sweetly, he said, 'I am full of admiration for the efficient way in which you carry out your duties; and what a splendid looking dog you've got there. Is Lessing still with Mr. Bern?'

'You know Mr Lessing?'

'Very well indeed.'

Goddard was relieved; the buck of making a decision could now be passed to somebody else. 'Well, if you have a word with Mr Lessing,' he said, 'he can say if it's O.K. or not.'

Lessing took a minute or two to answer the front door bell, he was busy with the ritual weekly silver-cleaning in his pantry. When he finally opened the door and, to his surprise, saw Hooky standing there with Goddard in close attendance, there could be no doubt about his welcome. Lessing had been with his master on the Madeira holiday and knew the high regard that Hooky was held in as a result of the famous deck-chair tidal-wave rescue.

'Why Mr Hefferman,' he said, 'this is a surprise. Mr Bern never told me you were coming.'

'He didn't know,' Hooky explained. 'Something rather urgent has cropped up. Or at any rate it may turn out to be urgent.'

'This gent's O.K. then?' Goddard asked.

'Quite O.K.' Lessing assured him.

Goddard nodded and began to move off. 'Thanks for your help,' Hooky called after him, 'and give Fido a biscuit from me for his tea.'

'It's Zena not Fido,' the security man told him, 'and she's a bitch.'

'I'm not surprised,' Hooky said. 'Is Mr Bern in?' he asked Lessing.

'Well, he is and he isn't as you might say, sir.'

'Presumably that means that Miss Cave is here?'

'You know Miss Cave, sir?'

'Only too well,' Hooky said adding as an afterthought, 'Or perhaps on reflection not quite well enough.'

'Well, it's true she is here, Mr Hefferman; and Mr Bern is up in the gallery with her,' the butler paused for a moment, looked Hooky levelly in the eye and added, deadpan, 'he often does go up in the Gallery with her.'

'And I expect you've got instructions not to disturb him?' Hooky asked.

'Being up there with Miss Cave he certainly wouldn't want to be disturbed in the ordinary way of things,' the butler said, 'but you turning up like this, Mr Hefferman, and telling me it's something urgent, why, that's rather a different matter of course. Perhaps you'll come in and wait in the hall a minute, whilst I go up and let Mr Bern know you're here.'

Inside a rather dreary hall Hooky said briskly, 'I'll wait here till you come down then,' and to give the impression that he meant what he said he seated himself somewhat ostentatiously on an extremely uncomfortable chair near the foot of the stairs. Six seconds later when Lessing had reached the half-landing and disappeared from sight Hooky jumped to his feet and cat-like, very cautiously and quietly, began to go up the stairs.

When Lessing was half-way along the corridor that led to the Gallery the door of the Gallery opened and Virginia Cave came out carrying a flat parcel. She was clearly startled at seeing the butler there; he had no right to be there, he ought to be safely tucked away in his pantry cleaning the silver. Virginia's throat contracted a little with apprehension.

'Is Mr Bern up here, Miss?' he asked.

'Up here?' Virginia shook her head. 'No. I've no idea where he is.'

'I—' whatever Lessing was going to say was cut short by a sound that jerked his head up in surprise and alarm—a sound of muffled shouting and fists hammering on a door.

'Whatever's that?' the butler demanded in mingled astonishment and alarm, for answer he had most of the wind knocked out of him as Virginia shoved him violently against the wall and pushed her way past him to run along the corridor towards the head of the stairs. What had brought Lessing up there so unexpectedly she couldn't imagine; but, once past him, she still had hopes of saving the day; it would take the butler a minute or two to free Bern and to sort things out with him, meanwhile there would be no trouble with Goddard and, since everything was being done to an exact time-table, Len would be waiting in the getaway car in Acacia Road.

All these agreeable hopes were blown sky-high when she reached the half-landing. The half-landing was small and a broad-shouldered man standing a few inches over six feet in height seemed to take up all the space there was. Virginia stared at Hooky in disbelief; he smiled back at her and shook his head sorrowfully.

'What the devil are you doing here?' she demanded.

'I thought I'd like to see how you were getting on with your copying.'

'Let me by at once.'

'Not just for a minute or two.'

'How dare you stop me?'

'You'd be astonished at the things I dare do where women are concerned,' Hooky assured her. 'What is all that rumpus upstairs? Anything wrong up there?'

'God damn you for an interfering bastard,' Virginia said bitterly.

Hooky smiled at her; but he didn't budge.

'That may well happen,' he said, 'but meanwhile I'm wondering what's in that parcel you're carrying.'

'I CAN'T get over it,' Julius Bern complained angrily, 'especially after the way I treated the girl.'

Hooky, who by this time had had a view of the millionaire's own particular little private collection of photographs and drawings, was brusque in his reply, 'Maybe it was the way you treated her that was the trouble,' he said.

Bern side-stepped this. 'She was actually stealing my picture. The van Dysen. *The Woman with a Flageolet.*'

'You'd have a hard job to prove she was stealing it. Her story is she had your permission to copy it and she was taking it back to her flat to make some final alterations to the copy she's making.'

'Who in God's name would believe that nonsense?'

'You'd be surprised at what a clever counsel can persuade a jury to believe.'

'And what about locking me in the little private gallery?'

'She locked you in there because she was shocked and disgusted at what she saw and because you suddenly assaulted her.'

'She's been in there half a dozen times with me and enjoyed it.'

'So you say. She'll say differently.'

'You sound as though you were on her side, Mr Hefferman.'

'I'm on the side of least said soonest mended. It's almost certain that she did intend to steal your van

Dysen. But the way things turned out you would have a mighty hard job to prove it in a Court of Law. What will be proved, if you're ill-advised enough to go to law, is that you are a dirty old man with one of the best collections of erotica in London and that you were busy corrupting a young woman by showing it to her—can you imagine the meal the Press is going to make out of that?'

'My God,' Bern exclaimed bitterly, 'I'll never get mixed up with a woman again.'

'That's a resolution I've often made,' Hooky told him, 'but luckily I've never kept it.'

'SO WHAT went wrong?' the Detective Inspector asked sharply.

'Just about everything as far as I can see,' Sergeant Fitt answered. 'I've a feeling the thing was there, if you know what I mean, but somehow we never got hold of it. The girl Cave came out into Acacia Road carrying a parcel just as we expected her to. Our two chaps were there and closed in at once. They thought they were bang on target, but when they got the parcel opened up there wasn't any picture there, just a piece of thin board, the sort of thing she might have had to protect a picture if she was carrying one—only, as I say, she wasn't; so what could they do?'

'What did they do?'

'Detained the girl whilst they questioned people in the house; but that didn't get them anywhere. Nobody was saying anything, well, not anything that helped anyway. No picture had been stolen and nobody had any complaints about anything, that was the general line. Our chaps had to accept it, but they didn't think it was true.'

'Why not?'

'It smelt wrong somehow, but there was nothing they could pin down.'

'What about the getaway car?'

'There wasn't one.'

'No getaway car? Has anybody checked on Len Carron?'

'Of course they have. He wasn't there, and a neighbour saw him loading suitcases into a car and driving off early this afternoon with a woman.'

The Inspector considered all this and finally said philosophically, 'Well, you've got to draw a blank sometimes, I suppose.'

'And there's another thing,' Fitt continued. 'This man Hefferman was there at Pine Place.'

'Your private eye pal? What in God's name was he doing up there?'

'Looking after Miss Virginia Cave presumably.'

'Looking after my backside,' the Inspector said testily. 'I've told you before, Fitt, these private eye merchants are just a pain in the neck, they do nothing but get in the way.'

VIRGINIA picked up the telephone and heard Hooky's voice.

'Are you going on persecuting me?' she demanded angrily.

'Don't talk gibberish, woman. Persecute nothing. I'm trying to save you from your stupid self.'

'I haven't the faintest wish to be saved from anything by you.'

'Perhaps you prefer old men with dirty minds.'

'All men have got dirty minds.'

'Maybe you've got a point there; but I wouldn't go round trying to steal pictures anymore if I were you.'

'Why not?'

'Well, for one thing, the Law takes a dim view of it.'

'I have nothing but contempt for the Law. What can the Law do to me?'

'Have you ever seen the inside of Holloway?'

'Now you are threatening me.'

'You do say some of the most ludicrously stupid things I've ever heard. All I'm doing is giving you a friendly word of warning.'

'Damn your friendly word of warning; and damn you.'

'And there's another tip—if you're in the market for tips.'

'I'm in the market for nothing, especially from you.'

'Steer clear of Len Carron. Len Carron's a villain.'

'And you're a saint I suppose, a smug, self-satisfied saint.'

'That's the first time I've ever been called that.'

'Leave me alone, Hooky Hefferman, get out of my hair.'

'Nothing could give me more pleasure,' Hooky lied. 'You go your own way to hell then.'

'I propose to do that very thing without any more interference from you please.'

'My God, you are a pig-headed stupid little bitch aren't you? If you get into trouble you can always give me a ring.'

'Like hell I will,' Virginia said and slammed the receiver down.

The conversation on the telephone depressed Hooky; he had hoped to make some headway with Virginia; there had even been moments during the past few weeks when he had thought that something might come to life between them. Now he had to realise that he had failed and that before long he would have to go to Eaton Square and say that he had failed. It was not a prospect that pleased him . . .

His henchman Roly Watkins came in with the evening paper. 'You're looking depressed, Mr H,' he said. 'You look down; the old trouble is it? Too much wine and too many women? What a gorgeous complaint to suffer from; you don't know when you're well off, Mr H.'

'The frail bark of good intent is shipwrecked on the merciless sea of feminine folly,' Hooky said.

'That wouldn't surprise me in the least,' Roly informed him, 'not in the least it wouldn't. Who said that? Your old Chinese pal was it?'

'Chu Ling,' Hooky admitted. 'Several centuries ago, and how right he was.'

'Well don't let it get you down, Mr H,' Roly said comfortingly, 'you can't win 'em all.'

The telephone rang and Hooky reached out quickly for the instrument. Ever an optimist he thought she'll have come to her senses, she'll say let's meet in The Good Soldier and call it a day, let bygones be bygones—

'Hallo there?' he led off cheerfully. But it was not a feminine voice that answered him.

'I've been trying to raise you all day but there's been no reply,' Nick said, 'aren't you ever in?'

Hooky said that one or two things had kept him busy and what did Nicky want?

'Those PBP shares you told me to buy; I don't know who gave you the tip but he certainly knew something. Since midday yesterday when the take-over by C.L.D. was announced the market has gone mad about them. I bought for you at seven p; do you know what the latest quotation is?'

'You tell me, Nick.'

'Forty-two p! Forty-two! It's fantastic. I don't know whether to advise you to sell or to hang on. I don't know what's happening.'

'Sell, Nick, sell. I'm not ambitious; by that sin fell the angels.'

'And God knows you're no angel. All right, you lucky so-and-so I'll sell and at forty-two you'll have done very nicely indeed, thank you.'

Hooky replaced the phone. Roly Watkins who had an insatiable curiosity about other people's telephone calls was still there.

'What was that last remark of yours Roly?' Hooky asked him.

'I said you can't win 'em all.'

'True enough,' Hooky agreed, 'but there are compensations. You can sometimes win some of them.'

MURDER
HAS A PRETTY FACE
JENNIE MELVILLE

MYSTERY
WORLDWIDE LIBRARY
TM

BACKLASH
PAULA GOSLING

Winner of the John Creasey Award for crime fiction

THE TASK THAT FACED GENERAL HOMICIDE SEEMED MONUMENTAL

They had four dead cops from four different precincts, all shot through the head. The headlines were screaming cop killer. Rookies were making sudden career changes, while veterans of the force were anxiously eyeing retirement dates. Panic was growing.

For Lieutenant Jack Stryker, the pressure was coming everywhere: up from below, down from above, and in from the outside. And with each new death, the pressure increased. Was the killer shooting cops at random...or was there a more sinister reason for the murders?

But when Stryker is hit and his partner is almost fatally wounded...Stryker knows it's time to forget procedure and put an end to open season on Grantham's finest...before he becomes the next trophy of a demented killer.

"Gosling's novels have all met with critical acclaim."

— *Library Journal*

Flight to YESTERDAY

VELDA JOHNSTON

A NIGHTMARE REVISITED

Dubbed a "young Jean Harris" by the press, Sara Hargreaves spent four years in prison for a crime of passion she didn't commit. Now she's escaped, and she's desperate to clear her name and to see her dying mother.

As her face appears nightly on the local news, Sara disguises herself, and with the help of a young law student she is forced to trust, she returns to the scene of the crime.

The fashionable sanatorium where handsome plastic surgeon Dr. Manuelo Covarrubias was stabbed with a knife bearing Sara's fingerprints looks much the same. But as Sara begins her flight to yesterday, the secrets surrounding the callous playboy doctor who jilted her unfold. Secrets that once drove someone to murder...secrets that could kill again.

A SENSITIVE CASE
ERIC WRIGHT

AN INSPECTOR CHARLIE SALTER MYSTERY